'Tis the Season
by Mike Broemmel

Published internationally by Pinnacle Books, Ltd.

© Mike Broemmel 2020

mike@mikebroemmel.com

This book is a work of fiction. Any similarity between the characters and situations within its pages and places or persons, living or dead, is unintentional and co-incidental. The author and publishers recognize and respect any trademarks included in this work by introducing such registered titles either in italics or with a capital letter.

Dear Reader,

'Tis the Season is released during the height of the Coronavirus Pandemic. The 2020 holiday season is likely to best be remembered not by families coming together to celebrate, but rather by many loved ones having to remain at a distance during this special time of year.

My hope is that the tales in this collection will provide a bright moment for you and yours no matter where you may be during this holiday season.

Mike Broemmel

Dedicated to the Memory of

Sister Jeremy Dempsey, OSB.

1925 – 2020

My English professor who told me to:

"Use your pen wisely."

Letters to Saint Nick

My wife and I retired to Miami Beach in the fall of 1960. We cast ballots for John F Kennedy from a voting booth set up in the lobby of the Eden Roc Hotel, a couple blocks from our snug bungalow just off Collins Avenue.

Our only son, his wife and our two granddaughters traveled from Kansas City to Miami Beach by train to spend Christmas and a winter vacation with us. Our older granddaughter was six and our younger just two.

On one afternoon early in the New Year, I sat on a bench at the beach with my older granddaughter. While looking out over the crystal Atlantic Ocean and enjoying a warm breeze, the little girl, done up in pigtails, asked me what I remembered about my favorite Christmas.

"That's easy," I thought to myself, and proceeded to tell her about Christmas 1932.

I turned thirty-two years old in '32 and was the Executive Vice President of August J Crosby Dry Goods Co., the department store founded by my own grandfather and ran by my father in a huge granite building at 12th and Main in downtown Kansas City, Missouri.

Since well before I was born, the Crosby store had a Christmas tradition of answering letters from children to Saint Nick. I explained to my granddaughter that Santa was such a busy person he needed help answering all the mail he received.

Right after Thanksgiving 1932, my father called me into his office to tell me he had decided I would be one of the people at the store assigned to answer Santa mail. I would spend every afternoon until Christmas writing back to children who had written to Santa Claus care of the store.

I can still remember how fiercely I protested.

"Oh, come now!" I exclaimed. "You can't be serious!"

My father said nothing in reply. He let me rant, rave and protest the assignment until I ran out of steam. He then said: "You start this afternoon."

I stalked back to my office, still fairly fuming with anger. I was the Executive Vice President of the Crosby Co department store. I did not want to be stuck writing letters to children.

At noon, a stack of a couple dozen letters from children was delivered to my office.

"Take these away, take these back!" I yelled at the hapless and helpless mailroom boy. I can still picture his horrified expression as he sprinted out of my office, leaving the letters on the edge of my desk.

I left the letters alone, intending to carry them down to the mailroom myself, unanswered, at the end of the day. I spent the remainder of the afternoon inspecting various departments in the store to make sure all was running smoothly in preparation for the holiday shopping season. I found myself still at the store, a couple of hours after closing, sitting alone in my office.

I idly picked a letter off the top of the stack just as I was preparing to leave. I read the child's missive to Saint Nick.

Dear Santa Claus,

My name is Rowan. I am nine. My Mama works. She works for some people at the Country Club Plaza. They are rich. We are not. They are white. We are not. For Christmas I would like a truck. The truck does not have to be new. Just a truck. That would be swell.

Your friend,
Rowan Washington
PS. Can you tell the people my Mama works for to let her stay home with me for Christmas?

I sat back down in the big, leather chair behind my desk. I wondered, even if I was going to answer these letters, what would I say to a boy like Rowan?

"Sure, Santa will bring you a truck. Maybe even a new one. And, if your Mama worked for me she could have a day off on Christmas to be with you," I thought. But I knew that neither of Rowan's two requests of good, old Saint Nick would come true.

Leaving the office that night, I left Rowan's letter on my secretary's desk, along with the envelope and the boy's return address. I wrote a note to my secretary:

Please see if you can find this child's mother and a phone number.

The next morning, I returned to work and my office. As always, my secretary, Margaret, was waiting for me with a cup of coffee. She also handed me a sheet of paper with a woman's name and phone number.

"What's this?" I asked. I didn't recognize the telephone exchange and had forgotten about little Rowan Washington.

"The name and phone number you asked me to find."

"Oh, right, right," I muttered, taking the piece of paper and my coffee into my office. A short time later I rang Rowan's mother's phone number, getting no answer. I imagined she must be at work, likely a maid or cook for one of the wealthy families who lived at the Country Club Plaza, based on what Rowan wrote in his letter to Santa. I tucked the slip of paper into the breast pocket of my suit jacket, intending to call the woman later in the day.

I paid no attention to the other Santa letters on my desk until the same mailroom clerk dashed in and out of my office just after noon making a deposit that doubled the size of my stack. Margaret poked her head into my office, grinning mischievously like a carnival barker.

"Keep yourself quiet," I said after which she withdrew, chuckling lightly.

Within the hour, I picked a letter off the top of the stack. The child wrote:

Hi, Santa!
It's me! I'm fine! I hope you are fine! Mommy is fine!
Daddy is fine! Billy is fine! My cat is fine!
XXX
Betsy Lou Spaine

"Now this letter I can handle," I thought. I yelled for Margaret to come into my office to take a letter. She appeared, still wearing the same wry grin.

"I don't take Santa letters," she advised. "You have to write them by hand." As she spoke, Margaret handed to me a stack of stationery emblazoned with:

Santa Claus
North Pole

I moaned as Margaret made her exit. Nevertheless, I took a piece of Saint Nick stationery and scribbled out a reply to Betsy Lou Spaine. I wrote:

Dear Miss Spaine:
I am pleased to hear of your family's good health.
Cordially,
Santa Clause

I did not realize that in my haste, I misspelled "Claus." I proudly trooped out of my office and dropped my response on Margaret's desk directly in front of her as if to say: "Take that."

Margaret looked at the letter and said: "Boss, this is a rotten letter. And you misspelled Santa's name."

She pulled a red pen out of a desk drawer and marked up my letter like a frustrated fifth grade teacher.

Shortly, I redid the letter to Betsy Lou, spelling corrected and to my secretary's satisfaction. Passing over the revised version to Margaret, I received a passing mark.

Curiosity got the best of me and I picked another letter off the growing stack on my desk.

Dear Mr Claus,

I am writing to you for both my sister, June, and I. I am ten. She is three. She cannot write by herself and Mom and Dad said I have to write for both of us.

I have been good this year, even though I am ten. My sister has been good because she is three.

Would you please bring me a baseball, a mitt and a bat? I want to play baseball and need these things to play.

Would you please bring my sister, June, a dollhouse? I guess some dolls, too. Okay?

Thank you, Billy Jones
670 31st St
Kansas City, Missouri

"Margaret!" I shouted, my office door being left open a crack for when I needed to call for my secretary. Entering into my office, she mocked me dryly. She had worked for my father and known me since I was a child.

"You bellowed?" she said.

"Go down to Sporting Goods. Bring me a couple of baseballs, a bat and a mitt that will fit a boy who is ten. Then go to Toys and bring me a dollhouse and couple of dolls."

Margaret saw that I had a Santa letter in front of me on the desk. But that did not stop her from saying something about "Playtime, Mr Crosby?"

When Margaret returned with the items I needed, we packaged them up and I had Margaret take them to the mailroom to be sent off to Billy Jones and his little sister June. I told Margaret to try to find a phone number for the Jones family on 31st Street to let the parents know the desired gifts from Saint Nick were coming.

I read and responded to a dozen more of the Santa letters on my desk, just like I did with Billy and June Jones. Wrapped up as I was in my doling out toys and gifts, I lost track of time. Margaret had left for the day and the sun had set.

I picked up the telephone and rang up little Rowan Washington's home, this time reaching his mother. After explaining who I was and mentioning Rowan's Santa letter, Mrs Washington provided me with the information I desired. Clicking off the line from the woman, I set about the task of creating a Christmas I hoped Mrs Washington and her boy would always remember.

The following day, I took lunch with Hubert Van Gibb. Hubert and I were students together at Maur Hill Prep during our teenage years. We met at 1:00pm at the Cattlemen's Club overlooking the freight district and stock yards.

Hubert reached the Club ahead of me and graciously stood at the table to greet me when I arrived. "What a nice surprise to hear from you last night," Hubert said as we sat down, referring to my phone call inviting him to lunch.

"It has been a while," I replied. "How's Estelle?" I asked.

"Very well. You know, bustling about for the holidays."

I nodded politely and he asked me how the store was doing. I asked about his wife, he asked me about the store. Never before had I felt more single, like the consummate bachelor, which I really had become.

We both ordered London Broils and gin martinis, two drinks apiece.

"Listen, Hubert," I said, halfway through our luncheon, "I understand you and Estelle have a cook named Mrs Washington."

10

Hubert eyed me suspiciously, probably thinking that I intended to hire his house help away from him.

"It's not what you think," I said, responding to my companion's droll expression. He took a sip from his thin martini glass and nodded for me to carry on.

From that moment, I rambled for over ten minutes, telling Hubert about the Santa letters coming to the store, how I really did not want to do the project – at first – and, I told him about the letter from Mrs Washington's son, Rowan. By the time I finished my tale, poor Hubert Van Gibb had no idea what I wanted of him, my remarks were so jumbled.

"What I want ..." I finally, flatly stated, "what I want is for you to give Mrs Washington Christmas Day off so she can be with her boy."

Before Hubert could object, or laugh in my face, I quickly told him I would arrange for full catering of Christmas dinner, whatever Hubert and Estelle wanted, the best of everything, from the Hotel Savoy. All free of charge.

Hubert thought for only a moment, and then shot his right hand across the table to shake mine. "It's a deal!" Hubert happily agreed.

Feeling pretty pleased with myself, I headed back to my office at the store. Whistling as I walked past Margaret's desk, she merely grinned, slightly shaking her head.

In my absence, another delivery of a couple dozen Santa letters had arrived and was sitting on my desktop. I wasted no time in diving into the new letters and the leftovers I had not finished previously. As with the day before, I lost track of time and ended up writing letters and gathering gifts until late into the night.

I decided to and did in fact arrive at my office very early the next morning, just after dawn, to go back to work on the Santa Claus mail.

The second letter I read that morning was from a little boy aged six.

Dear Santa Claus,

My name is Ricky and I just turned six. I live with my Momma. I don't have a Daddy.

My Momma and I live in a house just off the Farmers' Market. Our house isn't big and I'm afraid you don't know where it is. Momma explained to me last year that our house is hard to find, sometimes, and you not coming to visit wasn't because of me.

So, Santa, this year I drew up a map with this letter so that you will find my Momma and me.

My Momma works when she can up at the Hearty Perk coffee plant on Central Avenue in downtown. I just started the first grade.

For Christmas, I really don't want much at all. Just a football. That would be swell. But mostly, I'd like something for Momma. She is very pretty, you know, and she works very hard. If I could, Santa, I'd buy her a nice dress. The kind of thing the women wear when they go shopping downtown. She is just as pretty as they are.

My Momma, her name is Dahlia, just like the flower. So, Santa, if you can't bring the football, it is okay, but please follow the map and bring a dress for my Momma. Thank you.

Love. Your pal,
Ricky Nicks

Paper-clipped to the letter was a crude map evidently drawn by the boy himself, using red and green crayons.

I read Ricky's letter over once more and then yet again.

With the little Christmas colored map in hand, I dashed out of my office, passing my puzzled looking secretary in the hallway as she arrived at the store for the day's work. I did not give her the chance to ask where I was going.

Pulling my car out of the store's parking plaza, I sped through the downtown streets filled with the rush of people trooping to work. Even in the heavy traffic, I still managed to make the Farmers' Market in less than fifteen minutes. Following Ricky's hand-drawn map, I was on his street, a narrow dead-ender, and a few minutes later, I reached the house Ricky Nicks and his mother called home. A tiny patch of winter brown grass fronted the yard behind a fence of bent, rusting chain link. A small mongrel dog was chained to the remains of a tree, really a glorified stump, in the yard. The dog didn't bark or even stand up.

The house itself was tiny, having only a door and a solitary window on the front face. It looked empty at the moment and for a time, parked in front of the property, I found myself fighting a rigorous impulse to walk across the yard and sneak a peak in the little window.

Something about the boy's letter to Santa Claus led me to reckon that even though he and his mother were in dire financial straits their home would be warm and pleasantly comfortable inside, no matter how plain and simple.

I lost track of time, sitting in front of Ricky Nicks' house. An old, brittle woman deliberately walking near my parked car, scowling, caught my attention and prompted me to motor off back to the store.

I spent the remainder of the day picking out toys for Ricky Nicks. I then went to the Women's Boutique in the store to select some dresses and accessories for Ricky's mother, Dahlia.

"So, what size, Mr Crosby?" the boutique clerk asked me when I told her I desired a selection of nice dresses for a woman, for Christmas gifts.

I shrugged, having never seen Dahlia Nicks.

The clerk, an older woman, smiled. She was used to waiting on an occasional male customer shopping for a wife or a girlfriend. I did not immediately pick up on the fact that the sales clerk assumed I was shopping for a particular personal lady friend.

"So you don't know her size, then?" she asked.

"No, I guess I don't," I replied.

Trying to be helpful, the clerk asked how 'my lady friend' looked, size-wise, in comparison to her.

"You know," I honestly replied, not thinking the situation through fully, "I don't know what she looks like."

The sales lady frowned, indeed nearly grimaced.

I fumbled a confused semi-explanation after which I eventually retreated from the boutique, telling the puzzled clerk I would be back when I had some idea what size dress was needed.

Returning upstairs to my office, I found Margaret waiting, wearing an earlobe to earlobe grin and looking like a person who succeeded in a particularly mischievous prank.

"Maralee just called," Margaret said to me as I entered into my office suite.

"Who?" I asked, slowing my pace slightly although still progressing towards my private office.

"Maralee," she repeated in a manner making it clear that Margaret believed I most certainly knew a woman named Maralee.

"I don't know a Maralee." I brushed off Margaret as I side-stepped past her desk.

"You just talked to her," Margaret retorted as I prepared to shut my office door on her.

"I didn't just talk to her," I replied. "I just got back from the dress boutique." I shut my office door on Margaret, but not before I heard her begin to chuckle.

I reopened my door, only a crack, with an inquisitive look.

Margaret rolled her eyes. "Maralee is the clerk in the boutique."

In turn, I crossed my own eyes, exited my office and said: "Say …" I explained Ricky Nicks' letter to my secretary and my dress size dilemma.

"So, boss, you want me to guess for you?" Margaret teased, obviously pleased with my somewhat lighter mood in recent days.

"No," I replied, but I did ask if she would accompany me to the Nicks' house directly after work. I told her I would deliver some Santa gifts for Ricky and Margaret could estimate Dahlia Nicks' dress size.

Margaret protested a little, but then thought the better of her first instinct to refuse to accompany me. She realized the jaunt I proposed might be amusing. Certainly, she found the whole developing escapade to be out of what she perceived to be my common character. She agreed to tarry along with me that evening.

A few minutes after five, Margaret and I left the store and, once more using the red and green crayon map, headed off to the Nicks' house by the Farmers' Market. With us, we had the gifts for Ricky intended to be packages from Saint Nick on Christmas Day. And, Margaret had orders to look Dahlia Nicks over and see what size dress the woman likely wore.

Arriving at the Nicks' house, I saw a light glowing in the one front window.

"Here?" Margaret asked.

"Here," I replied, finding myself scanning up and down the block to see if the scowling old woman from earlier that day might be out and about. No one seemed to be stirring that chilly, November evening.

We both got out of my car, each with armfuls of gaily wrapped gifts. I looked at Margaret and saw that she was smiling. She, in turn, looked at me and said: "Boss, you're smiling."

Reaching the small concrete stoop, we juggled our loads to free up a hand between us to knock on the door. Giving up on that idea, I rapped on the door with one of my wing-tipped feet.

Promptly, the door opened and there stood a woman, a few years younger than me and a smiling boy with big, blue eyes.

"Hello," the woman greeted, at once matching the smile of the child at her side.

I quickly identified Margaret and myself, explained we were from the Crosby store and that Santa Claus asked us to lend a hand and help get some gifts delivered before Christmas.

"My letter!" the boy, Ricky, gleefully exclaimed.

Margaret, quick on her feet and knowing about the dresses yet to be delivered, wasted not a beat in explaining that there would be another delivery in a day or so.

Dahlia hesitated, pausing for a few seconds, then did in time invite us into the house.

Ricky wasted no time in relieving Margaret and then me of our burdens. He placed the gifts around the small Christmas tree in the corner of the living room. As I imagined while parked outside that afternoon, the house was simply decorated, yet warm, comfortable … lovely.

Dahlia Nicks had coal black hair, pulled back from her face with an ivory-colored clip. She wore no makeup, but rather had a rosy glow about her face. Dahlia's eyes seemed as dark as her thick hair. And her smile … her smile made her all the more beautiful. Within the minute, I realized – as did Margaret – that I was staring at Dahlia Nicks.

Margaret cleared her throat intending to cut short my intense gaze at Dahlia Nicks. I managed to look away at Margaret's prompting, but in no time my eyes were glued on the woman once again.

Dahlia offered us tea, which Margaret declined for both of us. Dahlia thanked us profusely for the gifts, making it very apparent that we had fulfilled her child's dreams for a merry holiday.

Feeling as if we overstayed our welcome, Margaret tugged on the sleeve of my suit coat. "We have to be going," she said.

As Margaret and I moved toward the door, I blurted out that I would be back the next day with more gifts.

"Gee, this is so swell!" Ricky happily exclaimed.

"Ricky!" Dahlia gently scolded. "Really, Mr Crosby …"

"Wayne," I cut in.

16

"What?" Dahlia asked.

"My name," I clarified. "It's Wayne."

Dahlia blushed. "Well … Wayne … You really have done more than enough."

I waved her off and assured her I would return the next day, at about the same time if that was acceptable to her. Rather than saying something along the lines of "That's fine," she seemed to carefully pick her words and said: "We'll be home."

Once back in my car, heading back to the store, Margaret said: "She's a four."

"What?"

"A four," Margaret said in a tone which indicated she was stating the patently apparent.

Not comprehending, I asked "For what?" and half expected Margaret to reply "For you." "A size four," she dryly stated.

"Oh, yeah. Right. Great. Maybe tomorrow you could help me pick out some dresses."

She nodded in agreement. Feeling as if I needed to make my actions all the more proper, I reminded Margaret that Ricky asked Santa for a dress for his mother.

"Of course," Margaret replied, a grin creeping across her lips.

When I arrived at work the next morning, I intended to take care of some more Santa letters. I found that I could not concentrate on that task or anything else. Dahlia Nicks, Ricky's mother, stayed on the tip of my brain since the night before.

The minute I heard Margaret enter our office suite, I left my office to meet her. Not letting her take a seat, I grabbed her by the arm.

"Dresses, Margaret, dresses."

I led her out of our office and down to the women's dress boutique. Margaret chuckled mischievously the entire way to the department.

She held her tongue while she helped me select half a dozen dresses that she thought would look nice on Dahlia Nicks.

17

Although she made no remarks in jest, I could readily tell from her expression that she was biting at the bit to rib me about what she perceived as my interest in Dahlia Nicks.

Repeating our ritual from the day before, Margaret and I wrapped more packages destined for the Nicks' household. With the gifts prepared, I spent the rest of the morning reviewing departmental inventory reports.

At noon, Margaret poked her head into my office.

"Need anything, boss?" she asked.

"Lunch," I replied.

"What would you like?"

"Let's say we go get lunch," I suggested. Margaret and I almost never ate together.

"Well," she said, piping up her voice.

"Well, let's go," I said, getting up from my desk.

I took Margaret to the Hotel Savoy for our luncheon. Over lobster bisque, Margaret brought up Dahlia Nicks.

"So, boss, tell me … What do you think of Dahlia Nicks?"

I verbally stumbled, like a high school freshman called to the blackboard. "What do you mean?" I finally managed.

She smiled, but in a kindly fashion, gentle.

"Well, boss, it seemed to me that our Dahlia Nicks strikes your fancy."

"Oh, gosh," I muttered, relieved that at least I did not say 'Aw, shucks.'

"She's a lovely girl," Margaret said.

"Well … I …" I could not escape the minor at the blackboard feeling.

Margaret rolled onward, pleasantly yet persistently.

"You should take her to dinner," Margaret finally pronounced with granite certainty.

"How is your bisque?"

"Take her to dinner." Margaret's course was well plotted and she was not to be detoured.

18

We finished lunch, returned to the store and went about our business for the remainder of the afternoon. At five, like the day before, I left for the Nicks' home over-loaded with parcels. On this trip, I went alone.

Dahlia, or perhaps Ricky, must have seen me walking up the cracked sidewalk to their house. They opened the front door just as I reached the stoop.

Dahlia, slightly smiling, nodded her head. "You really shouldn't have ..."

Before I could speak, Ricky spoke up. "He didn't. This stuff's from Santa."

Dahlia patted her boy's head and acknowledged that he was right.

Standing in the living room, Dahlia offered me some hot tea. "It's cold out there," she added.

"You know," I replied. "Tea, hot tea. That sounds great."

"Please," Dahlia said. "Sit." She pointed at an old sofa she covered with an afghan.

While Dahlia left the room for the kitchen to fetch the tea, Ricky sat down, Indian style, next to me on the sofa.

"Ain't Santa swell?" Ricky asked me, looking at the pile of wrapped presents under the tree. "And now I don't have to worry that he can't find our house."

I nodded, smiling at the little boy. I had an urge to give the young fellow a hearty hug.

"You know, I wrote Santa a letter and gave him a map I made myself so he wouldn't get lost. And best of all, he sends you early so I don't have to worry any more about Santa getting lost and not finding us, you know."

I had seen children in and out of our store every day. But, looking at Ricky, I could not recall ever seeing a happier child.

"That's right. I'm sure Santa just wanted to make sure you and your mom got your presents and that you did not lose sleep over him coming," I said.

19

"Here you go," Dahlia announced, returning to the living room with a pot of tea and a couple of cups and a frothy glass of milk for Ricky.

Over tea, Dahlia and I talked about Ricky and his schooling, Dahlia and her work at the coffee plant and now as a receptionist at a doctor's office. Dahlia was a proud woman and remained ill at ease about accepting the gifts I brought from the store, but she balanced her rightful pride against her son's obvious happiness.

I found myself losing track of time, a common occurrence for me those days. I finally apologized for staying so long after I had been at the Nick's home for over an hour. Standing to leave, I racked my brain trying to come up with another reason to make contact with Dahlia and her son.

"You know," I finally said, just before I opened the front door to depart.

"Yes?" Dahlia replied.

"The store …" I stammered. "The store also has arranged for Christmas dinner for you, Ricky and anyone else."

Dahlia pursed her lips, readying an objection.

"You've done more than enough."

"No, no," I responded, firming up my voice. "It's just part of what we do. We have dinner delivered to your house Christmas Day."

I made a mental note to call the Hotel Savoy to arrange for a second catered meal for the holiday.

With a little friendly arm twisting, Dahlia gave in and told me she was having her parents over to her home for Christmas dinner.

I bid Dahlia and Ricky a final goodbye and headed home, very light hearted. Although I resided alone in an apartment on the Country Club Plaza, I did not feel as if I lived in an empty dwelling.

After taking dinner, I bundled up and went back outside. The Spanish style buildings of the Country Club Plaza, an elegant shopping district south of downtown Kansas City, were all decorated for the Christmas holidays. Despite being in the midst of the Depression, twinkling lights decorated the buildings, a bright reminder that despite the hard times, good times could still be had.

I wandered around the Plaza for a couple of hours. Each time I passed by a couple walking arm in arm or hand in hand, I could not help but practically stare at them. Often we exchanged pleasantries as we walked on in our separate directions.

By the time I returned to my apartment, rather late at that point, I wanted to ring up Dahlia Nicks. I held myself, controlling my urge to telephone this woman I had just met lest she come to conclude I was knocked off my rocker.

The next morning at the office, Margaret wasted no time in asking me how my return trip to the Nicks' home had gone. I almost broke down and told Margaret what was on my mind, perhaps even in my heart. I suspected that Margaret was well aware of my feelings. Nevertheless, I ended up telling her that all went "Fine, just fine."

I did end up telephoning Dahlia Nicks that evening on the pretense of finding out what menu she had in mind for Christmas dinner. I phoned her again the following day, a Saturday, contending I had accidentally misplaced the original menu. And on Sunday, I called Dahlia again saying that we had not discussed dessert for the meal, even though I knew we had chosen pecan pie and whipped cream topping.

When Monday evening rolled around, I summoned enough courage to make a truthful telephone call to Dahlia Nicks. I spoke so rapidly, I was convinced that Dahlia did not understand what I had said when she replied, "Yes."

"You will?" I asked, surprised.

"Ricky and I would love to join you for dinner tomorrow night," Dahlia said, making it clear that she did understand what I had proposed, my invitation to her and her son.

The three of us dined together the following night and a full five more times before Christmas. Finally, Dahlia and Ricky invited me to join them and her parents for catered Christmas dinner at their little home.

"And that," I told my little granddaughter sitting next to me on the beach some thirty years later, "that was my most favorite Christmas, I do believe."

She played with the new toy in her hands and I looked out at the ocean again thinking of all the other wonderful Christmases in the intervening years. She looked up at me with eyes as blue and almost as wide as the ocean and said, very seriously: "You know, Grandpa …"

"What's that, dear?" I asked.

"My daddy's name is Rick," she said, adding, "And Grandma's name Dahlia."

"I know," I said.

The Pony Patch

Ma died, 1928. I was ten. We lost the farm, 1931.

I was thirteen then. I turned fourteen in November of that year; a month later Pa, my little brother, Zack, and my little sister, Sarah, Zack's twin, celebrated Christmas with Nanna and Pappa, Pa's folks. With Ma and the farm gone, Pa moved us to live with Nanna and Pappa in their three-bedroom house in Cedar Flats, Iowa.

The Depression hit Iowa like a burglar in the night. None of the folk in the county saw it coming. But when it hit, the Depression shattered homes and ripped through lives like a midnight bandit.

We were left with nothing. Our neighbors were left with nothing.

Folk lost city jobs, sure. But when the Depression broke in on us farm families, our pas lost work, but our families also lost our homes.

No Ma. No work, really, for Pa. No home.

But, Pa, Zack, Sarah and I were lucky – blessed to have Nanna and Pappa.

They didn't just take us in, they invited us home.

Plus, Pa landed some spot jobs; a day here, another somewhere else.

Nanna and Pappa, in their seventies, had no real savings to speak of. That may have worked out best for them as the Cedar Flats First Bank shut its doors for good way before most other banks. Pappa, like Pa, had farmed, retiring a few years before Ma passed.

Nanna taught school up until Pappa retired.

When they moved off the farm, they rented the place to the neighboring family, a ten-year deal. The monthly rent payments, that's what we lived on, all of us.

Pappa wished he could have held on to the farm a bit longer, he said that often.

Then, he would say, when the Cedar Flats First Bank took our farm, our home (before it shut its doors), we could have moved onto Pappa's and Nanna's farm and carried forth.

The twins, Zack and Sarah, turned nine on December 15, 1931, just before our first Christmas at Nanna's and Pappa's house in town.

Nanna, finding some fabric remnants somewhere, made a dress for Sarah and a shirt and britches for Zack. Birthday presents. With the sewing done, Nanna wrapped the garments in butcher paper she got from Hank's Beef Locker in town. She made ribbons out of corn husks. She made cards, one for Zack, one for Sarah, out of poster board, signing the handmade pieces: "Love Pa."

On the fifteenth, we celebrated the twins' birthday; they thought their swell new clothes, gifts from Pa, came from the big clothing store in Waterloo. Zack felt jaunty, Sarah a regal princess, as they tried on their seemingly store-bought outfits.

I noticed that Pa really did not smile much during the twins' birthday celebration around the kitchen table at Nanna's and Pappa's. I figured, at first, that he was stewing because the gifts for Zack and Sarah really were not from him, but were stitched up creations from Pa's mother. Then I figured he was worried about something else: Christmas was ten days down the pike.

I was sure he was wondering how he would get presents for the family. Although Santa was no longer a reality for me, Sarah and Zack were expecting a visit from St Nick. And how could Santa not pay a visit? The twins were good, very good, all year.

A few hours after the birthday party, we all turned in for the night. I shared a room with Pa since I was the oldest. Pa slept on one little bed, I took the other. Pappa tracked down the racks from somewhere, after we moved in, Pa, Sarah, Zack and me.

I was pretty certain Pa fell asleep before long, his breathing getting heavy. But, he did not sleep easy, tossing and turning from almost the minute he crawled into his bed. I imagined he was

24

dreaming, probably about Christmas and Zack and Sarah and Santa. He knew I was thirteen, his "little man" as he said. So, surely, he was not knotted up about me, too.

I closed my eyes, but no sleep came. I rolled over and over and over again, but I did not sleep.

"Christmas was ten days away," I thought. Still awake, I heard 'Pappa's clock', an old-fashioned grandfather clock, chime the midnight hour, each gong an effort for the ancient timer. Then, I thought: "Christmas is nine – only nine – days away."

Sometime after midnight, I drifted, finally, to sleep. I wondered if Pa and I had the same dream. Perhaps we did, we slept close enough to each other.

My dream of Christmas day was sad indeed, no visit from Santa and the twins could not understand why.
They were good, very good, all year long. But St Nick did not come with gifts or candy or anything nice and good. Nothing.

Pa woke at five, a habit from the farm with a dairy herd. I heard him crawl out of bed, his feet dropping to the floor, not hitting the boards with the same confidence I knew before we left the farm.

I stayed in bed a while longer until I heard Nanna join Pa in the kitchen, the sound of her dropping the old, iron skillet on a stove burner. In no time, I knew I would hear the sizzle and smell the scent of bacon and eggs frying.

Dressed in long-johns and a pair of huge wool socks, Pappa's, I walked into the kitchen, Nanna at work in front of the stove, Pa staring out the kitchen window. Maybe he looked at the glaze of frost coating the winter brown lawn. Perhaps he looked right at nothing at all. I could not tell for certain.

Taking a chair next to Pa, I said: "Frost, huh?"

He said: "Huh?"

He was not looking at the frozen dust.

"Frost. Outside," I said.

Pa tilted his head a bit, training his eyes directly to the ground.

"Uh-huh," he said.

25

We sat still and quiet for a few minutes more when Nanna put plates in front of us, bacon, eggs and biscuits.

Eating breakfast at Nanna's was how I imagined dining in a grand, uptown restaurant in the city, Waterloo. People came in to eat when they pleased, served up heaping portions of hot, tasty food. And then more folk would come in, get fresh plates, happily dine.

In the same way, Pappa and the twins came into the kitchen as Pa and I finished our bacon and eggs, Nanna prepared and ready to go.

On a school holiday for Christmas, I did not have to bundle up and troop off to the schoolhouse with the twins in tow. I decided to spend the morning reading a book, an adventure story. The twins dashed outside to play in the backyard. Nanna cleaned up after breakfast, Pappa and Pa sat with me in the parlor reading over yesterday's newspaper.

Every now and then, I looked up from my book, glancing from Pappa to Pa. Pappa, engrossed in the news, seemed oblivious. Pa at first appeared to be reading the portion of the paper he purloined from Pappa, and seemed intent on a particular story.

Eventually, I realized that while Pappa was going from page to page, taking in his section of the 'Waterloo Gazette,' Pa never turned a single sheet. Peering over the top of my book, casting my gaze directly at Pa, I soon saw that his eyes were not moving. He was not reading at all, only staring. He seemed to be holding the newspaper up as a shield, not as something to be read and absorbed.

"St Nick," I thought. "Pa's worried about there being no Santa Claus."

I tried to turn back to my book, the adventure story. But I could not keep my focus. I kept looking back up at Pa.

Finally, I set the book aside, put on my worn winter coat, a hand-me-down, and headed out the front door. Since moving to town, I liked to walk to the very end of Pappa's and Nanna's street when I needed to think. The road dead-ended at a place with a large house with peeling paint and many trees. But, most special of all, fronting the house was a little pasture and a little shed where the owner kept Shetland ponies.

I had never seen a beast like one of these ponies out on our farm. Cows, plenty. Horses, a few. But nothing like these little fellows.

Before moving into Pappa's and Nanna's house, we did pay regular visits. But I never explored the neighborhood until I ended up a real resident, a townie.

Reaching the pony patch, as I came to call the pasture point, I scrambled up to the top of the threeplank wooden fence, taking a seat. I don't know how long I watched the ponies walk about the yard, meandering in and out of their stable, when I realized someone was standing next to me on the roadway side of the fence. The man, older than Pappa even, finally cleared his throat to snag my attention. Startled, I nearly flipped off the fence and into the pony patch itself.

The old man reached out and snared me by the arm, probably keeping me from a fall.

"Whoa, there," he said, gripping my arm.

I turned to face the man, to thank him for keeping me in place. Before I could speak, my eyes met the old man's. He had green eyes like no color I had ever seen in a person's face. A Christmas-tree-green, deep, rich and large.

He was all bundled up in a thick woolen coat and a lambskin cap, leather gloves covering his hands.

He had a neat white beard, the color of downy, fresh snow. Most of all, the old man had a gentle, kind smile – how I imagined a fawn might look at his mother, the doe.

"Be careful, young man," the old man warned.

"I'm okay," I shot back, boyish defensiveness jagging my reply.

"Looking at the ponies?" the old man asked.

"Yep," I said, explaining that I often visited the pasture and the ponies.

"Good enough," the old man replied. "As do I," he added.

We talked a bit about this pony or that pony and I could tell that he really did spend time at the pasture. He knew at least as much about the characteristics of each animal as did I.

Before much time passed, I found myself telling the old chap about my family, our life on the farm and our move to town. I even went so far as to tell the man at my side about my Christmas worries, about Pa not being able to come up with Santa gifts for my little brother and little sister. I told the fellow that Sarah and Zack were good little kids and deserved a Christmas visit from St Nick.

The old man nodded as I spoke; I could tell he well understood. Finally, he said: "Always think the best thoughts and the best will come to you."

Like the man had done while I spoke, I nodded my head in turn, believing I understood what he said.

Shortly, the man bid his leave and walked off down the road in the direction of my grandparents' home. I returned my attention to the ponies, remaining on the fence for nearly another hour.

I went back home in plenty of time for lunch. The twins were pooped out from a morning spent at play in the yard.

We all spent the rest of the day inside together, Pa still distracted and distant. Before Pa and I turned in for the night, I told him of the man I met at the pony patch that morning. I told Pa what the man said, thinking it would cheer him up: "Always think the best thoughts and the best will come to you."

Pa smiled, tousled my hair and tucked me into bed.

The next week passed pretty quickly, Pa still sad looking throughout. During the week, I made a few more walks down to the pony patch, running into the old chap each time. I began to wonder if the fellow was watching for me to come see the ponies. I thought that perhaps the man lived in the house with peeling paint across the pasture from where I sat on the fence top to think.

He did not walk from the house when he came to me while I sat on the fence. And, I never saw the man walk to the house.

Through the whole week, I never learned the man's name, never thinking to ask.

I continued to share with the stranger with the soft white beard my concerns about Christmas, the twins and St Nick. Each time I explained my heavy heart, the old man listened, keeping the gentle smile on his face as if he understood exactly how I felt.

By the time Christmas Eve rolled around, Pappa had chopped down a hearty evergreen that Nanna had decorated in the parlor. During the afternoon of Christmas Eve, I overheard Pa and my grandparents talking in hushed tones in the parlor, standing by the tinsel covered tree. Like with the twins' birthday, Nanna said she had made some outfits for the twins, and me.

Nanna tried to convince Pa that the hand-tailored clothes would be enough of a gift from Santa for the children, considering the Depression and all. Pa was unconvinced and, based on the tone of his tired voice, very sad.

The conversation broke up when Pa ended up walking out the parlor door where he smoked a Prince Albert he rolled earlier. I joined Nanna and Pappa in the parlor. From the expression on my face, Nanna knew I'd overheard the discussion between the adults.

Nanna smiled at me and put her arm around my shoulders, with a fast squeeze; she bent over and kissed my cheek.

Pa stayed in the yard for what seemed like forever. A good part of the time he barely moved, looking like a wax statue I once saw at the Black Hawk County Fair.

All the while, the twins happily played in the backyard, jabbering cheerily about Santa's imminent visitation. I ended up taking a walk down to the pony patch, where I once more met up with the friendly gent.

"Good afternoon, young man," he greeted. As always, I did not hear the fellow approach. He just sort of seemed to materialize, appear from nowhere.

"Hi," I replied, happy to see him.

"How is your day?" he asked of me.

I shrugged.

"Still worried about your brother and sister and Santa?" he asked.

"Yeah," I said, looking down at the ground, feeling almost defeated, helpless.

"Remember what I told you?" he asked.

At the same time, the old man and I said: "Always think the best thoughts and the best will come to you." We both laughed at our simultaneous pronouncement, my heart suddenly feeling lighter, happy.

The old chap and I visited a while longer and then I returned home. Pa and the twins were back inside the house by the time I returned, Nanna hard at work getting Christmas Eve supper prepared. The twins were sitting, Indian style, in the center of the parlor floor making out a note for Santa that they would leave out with milk and cookies before going off to bed.

Pa actually looked a bit lighter; however, I could tell his lack of St Nick gifts still weighed heavily on him.

Just at six we gathered around the dining table and feasted on Nanna's glazed ham, marshmallow garnished yams, and peas with sweet onions. Plates cleared, Nanna served piping hot slices of pecan pie with fresh whipping cream.

After our meal, we went into the parlor, Pappa lighting a cozy Christmas fire. At first the twins objected to flaming out Santa's port of entry, but Pappa explained the chimney and fireplace would be well cool before the good fellow arrived.

Together we sang some carols and then Nanna told us the story of the first Christmas, Jesus' birth. Before she finished, before the Magi arrived, the twins were fast asleep on the sofa, one to the right and one to the left side of Pa.

Pa and Pappa carried the twins off to their beds. Although I wanted to stay with the adults a while longer, my eyes were heavy. Nanna prodded me off to my own room while Pa and Pappa tucked in Sarah and Zack for the night.

I slept sound and steady all night, waking just after dawn. Nanna was already at her morning post in the kitchen, I heard her moving about. Pa, out of his bed and out of the room, likely rose more than an hour earlier.

Unexpected, however, was the gleeful trill of the twins, happy in the parlor. Sitting up in my bed, I was surprised to hear the twins sound so merry, knowing that our Christmas gifts from Santa were going to be thin.

In an instant, I heard the sound of the quick patter of the twins' tiny feet speeding towards my bedroom. Popping through the door, Zack exclaimed: "Come quick!"

And Sarah added: "Santa's come!"

Each of the twins grabbed one of my hands, pulling me out from under my covers. Wasting no time in pulling through the kitchen and into the parlor, the twins positioned me to face the front window and the brightly adorned holiday tree. I focused on the tree, and the three small parcels underneath, one for me, one for Zack and the third for Sarah. I was puzzled by their excitement over the little, yet to be opened gifts.

"Not there, silly!" Sarah snapped, directing my attention away from the base of the evergreen.

"There!" beamed Zack, pointing out the parlor window into the front yard. Glancing about the room just before I took a look out the window, I saw that everyone was looking out to the lawn in front of the house.

Outside, safely hitched to the trunk of a bare oak tree in the yard, was a little pony with a rich red Christmas bow tied about his neck.

"Santa came!" exclaimed Zack.

31

"Santa came!" Sarah echoed, happily.

Nodding his head, as if in disbelief, but with a broad smile on his face, Pa whispered, "Santa came …"

We ended up keeping the Christmas pony in the pasture at the end of the road, which turned out to belong to a widow woman named Mary Claire Windsor.

We named the pony Penny and in the spring she gave birth to twins so each of us ended up with our very own pet.

No matter how often I ventured down to the pony patch, I never again saw the kind man with the downy white beard and the Christmas green eyes. I missed seeing the old soul. But, I knew in my heart, on that Christmas so long ago, St Nick paid a visit that I would never forget.

"Always think the best thoughts and the best will come to you."

The Breakers

I found myself on the ocean-side shore of the Isle of Palm Beach in 1963, sitting alone in tan colored, fine sand. Aged thirty-six then, six years prior a writer of bountiful acclaim.

In the mid-1950's I stumbled upon the story of a man, a wealthy chap, in a grand mansion on Palm Beach. I took that tale, put it to paper, created a novel I called my own.

Success, for me, followed. Fame, for me, came. Riches, for me, flowed.

"Not since Fitzgerald," one critic blew. Another: "Quite like the old man, Hemingway..." And one more: "The literary golden boy..."

The late afternoon recline on the beach marked the end of my first day on Palm Beach. Although I wrote of Palm Beach in my extolled piece, I had never been to the Island. Although I based the perilously flawed protagonist in my novel on the person of Dash Blaire, I never met the poor soul.

The sun would soon set somewhere far off in the West behind where I sat. The slate gray water of the Atlantic, especially churned, violently slammed in viscous breakers. After sitting in the sand but a short time, I designed that the ocean, deep and dire, cared nothing about those who made contact with its great waters. The ocean cared not a bit for the sailors and whalers and fishermen whose lives it claimed year after year after year.

The Atlantic was even indifferent to the innocents swept from shores into its cold heart, ripped by waves from off the land then into lonely, forlorn, watery graves.

Sitting next to the shoreline, the waves pounding a wicked beat, I determined that evening that the ocean cared nothing about all sins on the land as well, sins of commission and sins of omission. I imagined the menacing, brewing Atlantic waters would be my undoing, be my penance, and become my place of final repose. But the swelling waters would be non-plussed by my absolute act.

When the sun finally slipped from its day perch, I found myself shivering in the face of the uncaring sea. I shook, not because of the cool breeze, for the night, though in December, was most fair, pleasant. I quivered with angst, fearful of the bellicose waters rushing before my place on the beach.

With the gloom of night gathering around, I picked myself off the sand and hurried away, knowing full well that I would soon return. I fetched my auto, a Spartan winged Chevy, painted dull gray, a color that I believed best demonstrated the condition of my timid heart. Having arrived in Palm Beach that day after a leisurely weeklong trek down from Winchester, Virginia, I took a suite at The Breakers Hotel, a pinnacle point in the golden tone city. With its prominent twin towers, perfectly groomed garden ways and gilded ceilings, The Breakers courted the Kings and Queens of The Season since rising from its own ashes in the roaring age of Zelda and F. Scott. The Breakers alone was a Phoenix in a city that did not otherwise allow resurrection.

The finality of playing out on Palm Beach is what drew me to the place that brought me success, the place I'd never been, that Christmastime.

I reached The Breakers shortly past six and went directly to the well-appointed and well occupied pub I spotted as the bellman led me across the main floor after registering earlier that day. Despite the abundant number of comers, the pub was placid, serene if compared to the workaday gin holes I frequented back home in Virginia.

Around the perimeter, courtly gentleman engaged in gracious games of chess, with idle crystal glasses of Scotch whisky, neat, perched at their sides. Women, resplendent in jewels and soft silk, sat together in tidy clutches of three, sometimes four. Whispering as if in a blessed cathedral, the ladies took delicate sips of rich wine from long-stemmed glasses, chalice-like vessels to be sure.

34

A few ill-fitted stragglers sat round the bar on stools that were more easy back recliners on stilt-like legs. Tourists, I imagined, visitors, most likely. Certainly strangers to The Season.

I took my place, as if pre-assigned, at the bar leaving two plush stools between my nearest neighbor and myself. The tender on duty spared not a second in presenting himself. He immediately inquired if I was a guest of the hotel, a polite way of finding if he could tab me out to a room at the inn, or if he was facing a touring sight-grabber – "Cash, please, up front."

"I'm here," I said, my voice cracking. I had not spoken at all since providing my name at the front desk upon arrival hours earlier. I ordered my poison, gin and a splash of tonic water. The barman managed to prepare my simple drink with noticeable flourish.

With my drink served, I cautiously turned to look behind my shoulders, first to the right, then off to the left. At my favorite Winchester, Virginia, haunt – The Cork Street Tavern – a stranger was targeted for stares, accompanied by muttered commentary to and fro. No one at all looked in my direction. I determined that, at The Breakers, perhaps in all of the Isle of Palm Beach, I was a fragile specter at best but, most likely, invisible all together.

My first thought halfway into my second drink was to ask my outwardly pleasant and decidedly courteous bar man if he knew of Dash Blaire. I caught myself, knowing full well that he certainly knew of Dash Blaire. What I really wanted to know was how the man fared. But, rightly so, I held back.

I envisioned that if I uttered the name – "Dash Blaire" – the sullen gents and comely dames gathered about the pub would change composure in an orchestrated movement. Together they'd band and carry me off to the night-blackened ocean directly behind the grand hotel. There, at the tide breakers, my end finally would come. But I was not ready for my finale, at least not yet.

Well into my third gin, I paid a spot more attention to the man seated to my left, clad out of theme, dressed in Bermuda shorts, dark socks and sneakers. Emblazoned across his chest, in crimson stitching, was "Sunshine State." My guess was that the fellow regularly scanned about the pub himself. Consequently, our eyes met, contact made.

"Where y'all from?" he asked, leaving me to conclude that he called Mississippi, Alabama, Georgia or a Carolina home. Before I could respond, he volunteered: " 'Course, I'm from up Georgia way."

"Of course," I said, finding myself responding in a whisper while my bar side neighbor spoke in full, flush tones. I muttered, mumbled nothing further.

"So?" he prodded, intent on hooking me into a conversation I did not want to have with him.

"Virginia," I softly replied, feeling like raising my forefinger to my lips and to give the fellow a librarian's "Shh."

"Well I'll be a pickled plum," he spouted, certainly blowing spittle from his mouth, I was sure, although I could not see such an expulsion in the serene, soft lighting.

Most definitely convinced the Georgian and I were targeted with icy stares, I looked over both my shoulders and about the pub a second time. The women continued their prim patter, the men their slow moving games of chess.

'Invisible,' I thought, and grateful to be at that moment.

"A Southerner just like me!" the Georgian extolled.

A man of the South I was not. I moved to the Shenandoah Valley, to the town of Winchester, some eighteen months after the book, the piece that brought me fame, hit the New York Times bestseller list. I needed, felt I needed, to escape my former home in Baltimore. Wanting to vanish, I picked the most rural spot I thought I could stand, survive: Winchester, Virginia.

"No," I muttered in response to the Georgian's seeming call to a Confederate brotherhood between us. I looked closely at the man, for the first time, and felt a pang in my gut – pity, sorrow, grief – I was not certain. The Georgian, probably about my age,

36

had thinning hair and a fleshy, growing paunch. No wedding band. I gathered his venture to South Florida was a life-long dream. The eagerness in his pale blue eyes made me think of a runty boy picked to play a kickball game for the very first time.

And I ached. Either for the Georgian's innocence or, more likely, for the innocence I lost – no, intentionally abandoned – some several years past.

"So where y'all from?" the Georgian asked of me. "I mean, original like."

"Maryland, Baltimore," I replied, realizing I likely had more common roots with some of the chess playing men and chatting women in the pub than I did with my fellow sojourner. Likely at least a few were Easterners, either retirees to the island or Seasonal Residents. Certainly none of them were "from up Georgia way." "Whoa!" the Georgian spewed, I imagined with another spittle splatter.

The bartender happened to be looking my way, not because of an attraction to my patchy discourse with the Georgian but out of crafted routine. The time was ripe for the gracious server to see how my beverage was holding out. As it was, I was ripe for a refresher. I tapped the rim of my glass. Behind the bar stand I heard the barkeep's heels click to attention, ready to serve.

"I'm Hoyt." The Georgian had a name. "Hoyt Crump." The name of the Georgian so fastly fit, I imagined his parents waited until they saw their progeny garbed out in Bermuda shorts, dark hosiery, canvas shoes and a "Sunshine State" shirt before his Christening. On the other hand, perhaps, the Georgian Mr Crump was spawned by dastardly insightful folk, a man and a woman blessed with what a Hindu might consider a most clear third eye.

"Hello," I mumbled, knowing quite fully I was to tender my own name to jolly Mr Crump. I did not. I could not.

Having authored the book with a doom-destined character stylized after the island's very own Dash Blaire, and patently so, if my name were uttered at The Breakers pub, my invisibility would surely cease. There I would sit, like a dumb duck snuggling at the hunter's blind.

Mr Crump kept his earnest pale blue eyes trained on me, wanting my name.

"Oh," I fumbled.

Mr Crump smiled a toothy, aimless grin.

"I'm Ernest Fitzgerald," I lied, slapping together two of the century's most noted. Mr Crump thought nothing unnatural of my fictitious creation. A reader he most likely was not. On the other hand, I remained invisible, no-one else thereabout taking note of my patently conjured name.

Mr Crump reached across the two-stool abyss that separated us thus far, his chubby white fingers aiming for a shake. Masking my reluctance, I obliged.

"Good to meet'cha," he said, over-gripping my digits and pumping my arm with unnecessary effort.

"Yes," I replied, my left upper lip turning up in a vain attempt at a cordial smile.

I became certain the handshake would continue had the time not rolled around for the rhythmic bartender to approach Mr Crump to determine whether a beverage follow up was in order.

"Heck yes!" Mr Crump near blathered, his speech noticeably affected by whatever booze he'd ingested, for however long he imbibed. I noticed, for the first time, that Mr Crump ran a tab. I caught myself knitting my brow, surprised that the visitor from up Georgia way was a guest at the hotel.

Surely this was a once in a lifetime trip for Mr Crump. Returning my attention to my own cups, I realized this was a once in a lifetime visit for me as well.

I finished my drink, signed off my tab, bid the server and Mr Crump a good night. I ambled through the main floor, slowly making my way to the lift. I paid near complete attention to the ceiling, which I decided looked more like a cathedral's expanse as opposed to a hotel's cap. The 'Ceilings of The Breakers' lobby level were vaulted and minutely adorned, perhaps most like a church of Byzantium heritage. For the moment, I there resolved that seeing a man dropped to his knees in contemplative prayer would not have seemed unordinary, extraordinary.

The sense of church jogged my ginned head that Christmas was but two days hence. My Floridian trip, though not a holiday pass, was purposeful nonetheless. Walking through the still corridors of the grand hotel, I resolved to fulfill my journey's intent the next day. A foggy sense of propriety led me to reason that my intended handiwork needed to complete before the anniversary of Christ's birth.

Reaching the lift, I directed the costumed operator to floor five. The man merely nodded, seemingly sensing that I did not want to share even the slightest, simplest conversational exchange. At the door to my suite, I wasted not a beat disengaging the lock, entering and preparing for sleep. I rang the desk to set a morning wakeup call for 5:30am. My only plan for the morning was to see if the ocean was any less brooding at the dawn.

I surprised myself by being able to fall into a fast, dreamless sleep in short speed. The morning call from a cheerful lobby clerk seemed to come in no time.

Groggy, I asked the chipper woman who broke my slumber to have a pot of coffee sent around to me as soon as possible. I finished a shower just as a carafe of fresh Java arrived. I poured a cup, retreating back to the bathroom to shave.

Looking at the face before me in the heavy-framed mirror, I never would have imagined that the person of the reflected image was only thirty-six years of age. The face before me, the reflection of myself, had slack skin, pale to the point of nearly being a pallid aqua. Darkness encircled both eyes, eyes which seemed more like place holders than visionary portals let alone windows to the soul.

Not being able to bear the illuminated sight any longer, I quickly lathered and dispensed with my day-old stubble. I hurried out of the bathroom, clad in a hotel courtesy robe, sat on a sofa and took a second cup of coffee.

Dressing fast, I soon departed the hotel. Taking my plain gray car, I drove back to the same point on the beach I occupied the evening prior.

The sun just breached the horizon line formed by the flat Atlantic waters miles off when I parked and walked onto the beachfront. The ocean water at the shoreline calmed overnight. Rather than the fearsome breakers of the prior eve, the sea lapped – lapped onto the sand, sounding a soothing call.

Had I not recognized the beachfront specifically itself, I would have thought I was facing an entirely different ocean that morning, a sea far less the terrible judge I envisioned the Atlantic of the past eve. Perhaps I could imagine I was on the banks of the Indian Ocean and not on Palm Beach to undertake my intended deed, really deeds – two tasks that I needed to complete.

The sense that I must finish my journey's intent before Christmas dawned left me only what remained of the day. Therefore, I recognized that I could not dally at the shore and visualize places well away from Palm Beach. I had to soon depart and address my first task.

Standing shore-side, I was not sure which of my required personal assignments would be toughest, the first or the second – the latter when I returned to face the infinite finality of the watery expanse that lay before me that Christmas Eve.

So intent was my focus, internally on the tasks ahead while externally on the ocean now so blue, I did not see the very old looking woman approach from the right side of where I stood. The improbability of my not seeing her at once was compounded by the fact that the lady's movements were so labored. She stopped walking every couple of steps to take in deep, recovering breaths.

I nearly tumbled forward towards the water when the old woman said, before I caught sight of her: "I know you."

I immediately felt my skin flush, as if overcome by some exotic fever. Instinctively, I wiped my brow although I was not beading any sweat.

I glanced to my right, looking down at the old woman who was very small. She did not even top five feet in height and her weight was such that I belived on the spot if a breeze puffed up she would blow to sea.

Before I even realized I was staring at the lady, and not responding, she repeated: "I know you."

Her face was blank, wrinkled and brown but devoid of any obvious emotion. She did not look angry, sad, or pleased to be in my presence. She did not appear accusatory. Her bearing did not indicate that she recognized me as the fellow who flushed out a fictionalized version of Dash Blaire, exposing the soul of Palm Beach in a manner well remembered by the island's residents, certainly.

I nodded, my knees nearing a buckle because I found myself a writer short on words, unable to speak. The aged lady was not deterred by my silence, and thus unstable posture.

Once more, she began: "I know…"

But this time as the said "you", I managed a faint, "me."

She nodded. For a moment, uncertain and finally fleeting, I hoped she perchance merely had mixed me with an island resident. Perhaps she confused me with a fellow she met marketing or a chap who commiserated with her at Sunday church or Saturday temple. But, a few heart beats later, this optimistic possibility slipped away.

Clearing my throat, I finally asked: "You do?

Instantly, she responded affirmatively. Uncertain which of the sundry emotions that flooded my being was most apropos, I looked back over the water not knowing what to feel, let alone do or even say.

Undaunted, the woman flatly stated that I was the writer of that book, "that story pretty much about Dash Blaire, even though you changed his name. We all knew it was Dash Blaire." I nodded, barely.

"I know," she responded, adding softly: "And, after the story you made, Dash Blaire nearly killed himself, so I heard." Taking in a couple laborious breaths of salty morning air, the old women recommenced her slow trooping across the beach, carrying on in the same direction that led her to me in the first instance.

Not daring to let my gaze follow her snail-paced exit, I kept my eyes trained on the tranquil morning sea. Nonetheless, at that very moment my gut wrenched and I nearly spewed onto the unblemished sand. Bending at my waist and bowing forward, I breathed in the damp air slowly to calm my enflamed nerves and tossing belly.

I left the beach with deliberate haste. Reaching and starting my auto, I set off on the ten-minute motor trip to the home of Dash Blaire.

Reaching the Blaire residence, a Gargantuan manse, Spanish in treatment with a lightly pink glaze, I parked directly next to the gate. As if a caller was expected, which seemed unlikely because of my fictional adaptation of the owner's life, the gate itself stood open. I then reasoned a home, a house without visitors, did not need a closed fence to keep people out. Alarms, certainly, to keep burglars and nighttime predators away. But, not a closed gate, not a sealed fence line.

I removed myself from my car, cautiously. I found myself maneuvering not in a manner of a gentlemanly chap on safari. No, rather, I moved as a person making to a shrine, perhaps a tomb.

Standing directly in front of Dash Blaire's residence, the first paragraph of my best selling book bulleted through my brain, hotly and with wicked intensity.

"Regal royal palms stood sentry about the grand mansion, guarding Dabney Bloom in his unseemly pursuits."

Never having actually laid eyes on Dash Blaire's residence until that day before Christmas, I shuddered when I caught sight of royal palms growing serenely about the grounds.

Peering about the property from my standpoint outside the gate, my thoughts regarding the whole affair crystallized like never before – simply. The book, my book, had forever bound me to the man, Dash Blaire, and he to me as well. The pages I wrote forever changed the life of one Dash Blaire and my own, so solitary, as well. And for all of that, I needed to atone. As if pulled by magic, a mysterious spell, I found myself moving mystically up the cobblestone drive and in the direction of the front door. Although I moved at a turtle's pace, I suppose, everything around me seemed to fuzz and blur as if I were piloting forward in a speeding racer.

A seeming eternity passed before I reached the set of steps leading to the main entrance of Blaire's mansion. The strange slowness of passing time combined with the hurly-whirl of images as I walked took me to think of what it might be like to pass from one of Dante's levels of Hell to another.

Taking the steps I found myself poised to ring the bell, formally announce my presence. Instead, I spun around, violently, as if in looking at the tremendous door I stared into the eyes, the heart of some dire beastie.

I found myself taking air like I had done earlier on the beach when I felt I might let loose of my stomach. Shortly, my deep, deliberate breaths were replaced by an unseemly panting, like an overtaxed dog struggling to relieve impossible heat.

I forced myself to focus, to fine line my eyes onto something to sooth my ragged composure. Surely if I did not promptly do so, someone inside the house would spot me on the porch, gasping for air, perhaps even Dash Blaire himself. Such a turn would make my visit to the premises even more peculiar, outlandish, than walking to the door and chiming in my presence.

I moved my eyes from flower bed to flower bed. The swirl of gay coloring did bring me a slight sense of calm. I took some comfort in knowing these garden plots would be unbothered and unchanged by both tasks I needed to undertake that day.

Inhaling deeply, and holding the air, I turned to face the door once again. Wasting not a spot of time, I rang the bell.

Money was not what Dash Blaire lost because of my literary dalliance into the man's life. The well manicured grounds and the meticulously cared for manse itself paid testament to his enduring wealth. As a result, I expected the door to be answered by a servant in the employ of Dash Blaire.

Instead, when the door drew inward and open, there standing before me was the poor soul himself, Dash Blaire.

"I know you," he said, in the identical, nondescript tone used by the tiny, old woman at the beach less than an hour earlier. And, just as before, I found I could not speak. Handed a paper pad and an ink pen, I would not have been able to write either, for that matter.

Realizing I still held my breath, I gasped tremendously, startling Dash Blaire so much that he backed away, letting loose of his grip on the door's knob.

I should have apologized, at least begun to explain my presence if not myself. However, there I stood heavy like a large fall cabbage.

Dash Blaire broke the silence by saying: "You're the…"

Before he finished the phrase, we both said "Writer" in unison, although I spoke barely at a whisper.

Dash Blaire's expression registered "Why?" I could imagine he wondered at the moment not only "Why are you here?" but also "Why did you write … that book?" Certainly, with my very presence on the man's porch, the old wound of "Why did you write … that book?" had to have torn well open for Dash Blaire.

I found myself shifting my weight from leg to leg, although Blaire did not seem to notice. His eyes had not left my face since he'd opened the door and realized who was coming to call.

I had seen photographs of Blaire in the past, but none that I could recall viewing in the last few years. His face looked like I recollected from the photos. But his hair, Dash Blaire's hair was snow white. In the relatively natural course of aging, Blaire was too young, even then, to have cotton colored hair.

I naturally concluded that the unusual whitening of his crown was one of the various and sundry indignities he suffered following the publication of my transparent book. Nerves, I imagined. I had heard that bad nerves cause hair, sometimes, to lose its coloring. Havoc undoubtedly was visited upon Dash Blaire's entire constitution after what the chap endured following my bestseller's release.

I tried to avert my eyes from Blaire's snow white hair, not wanting the man to think I was staring at his crown.

Both of us continued to stand facing each other, no word passing between us.

Finally, Dash Blaire asked what, in light of the situation, was a logical query.

"Are you lost?"

I readily discerned that Blaire worked with effort to evenly modulate his voice, although he only spoke three syllables. He struggled to speak; I could not yet speak at all. I stiffly shook my head in response to his question.

Even though I answered Blaire's question by shaking my head in the negative, I wondered for the moment if I should have replied in the affirmative. Lost, I truly was that Christmas Eve in the late morning.

Dash Blaire's eyelids began to narrow, giving indication that his expression was changing. No longer did he bear a puzzled, perhaps confused look of "why". He began to look irritated, finally angry.

45

"What do you want of me?" Blaire, speaking firmly, asked, his rich brown eyeballs barely visible through his lowered lids. I imagined he thought of following up with: "What more do you think you can do to me, sir?"

I focused my brain works onto my lips and throat, but I could discharge not a sound.

Blaire might have well said: "Speak up, speak out or be gone."

The grip of his leaden lids over his eyes lessened appreciably. I wondered for the moment if he had found relief, perhaps satisfaction. I thought I saw even a happy glint in his more opened eyes. Perhaps Dash Blaire thought: "Aha, the man who so menaced my life with a tale, so wicked, is at a loss ... lost for words."

I wanted to state, convincingly to the fellow: "Sir, I am sorry."

But nothing, nothing at all, could I there emote. And so, like a child dashing from a fright, I turned from Mr Blaire and ran from his porch and out of his yard. Regaining my gray auto, I sat behind the wheel, not moving, for quarter of an hour. I dared not look back at the blush pink colored house with its royal palm trees standing guard.

Finally, wearily, I ignited my car's engine and returned to The Breakers Hotel where I would wait the coming of night. With the dusk I could then finish the last of my tasks for the day, all well done before Christmas. On this return to The Breakers, I did not dally in the lobby nor sojourn in the pub. I, in haste, took the lift back up to my suite where I waited out the remains of the day.

At twilight, I departed The Breakers and returned for the third time to my marked spot on the beachfront. With the most deliberate steps I managed all day, I walked towards the rushing breakers of the growing tide. The water, no longer blue colored as at the dawn, had turned back to the steel gray of the night before.

My task, numbered two, obliged me to carry on walking out into the water, beyond the point the merry swimmers played during the day. My life's final chapter would be played out in the dark

46

waters of the night, ending the past as I had obliterated the life of the main character in my book based on Dash Blaire's life.

Nearly to the point of my final resolve, I heard the pat-pat-pattering of someone coming across the sand from my rear. I decided to stop walking toward the water as if to admire the black beauty of the night. The trailing party likewise stopped moving, although I hoped the person would have walked on somewhere else.

I glanced behind me, focusing enough to determine that the person behind me was a man. I took a couple more steps towards the water and the man followed suit. When I rested once more, he also stopped walking.

On this occasion, I decided to maintain my post and not walk any farther until the other man retreated or carried onward somewhere else. I was not prepared to stand pat a long time, but that ended up being the reality.

Finally, after about a half hour, the stranger behind me started to move, in my direction. I kept my head trained out over the water so that the man's eyes and mine would not meet when he drew near. I listened, intently, as his footsteps grew louder, the man growing all the closer. And then the sound of the man's shoe soles plodding through the sand beach stopped, the man standing right next to me on the shore.

He spoke: "I followed you…"

Before he could finish his statement, I turned to face the stranger as he concluded: "… since this morning." Next to me, on the beachfront, stood Dash Blaire. He spoke on:

"I was right here, standing where you are, on the night your book hit the stands."

He paused for a moment, and then said: "I, like you, was a broken, ruined man."

Again he paused as I turned away to face the water ahead. Dash said: "I, like you, was going to walk …". His voice trailed off and he pointed to the black water of the ocean before us.

47

Barely above a whisper, Dash Blaire concluded by saying: "At the last minute, I chose to live. And so, sir, should you."

Dash Blaire spoke no further, raised no commotion. He quietly turned around and walked back across the sand to his life in Palm Beach, be it as it was at that time.

I waited until the man was well out of sight, although I wondered if he kept me somehow in view. I turned away from the ocean's water before me. I, too, started back across the perfect sand, away from the sea.

I finally sat down, for the third time, at my favored spot on the beach. I sat in the fine sand, all of the night.

Christmas Day dawned over the ocean with a majestic burst of the sun above, breaching in shards of yellow, orange and gold the horizon of the night.

On that Christmas Day, like Dash Blaire, I chose to live.

Snowy Night

The trio kept singing "Auld Lang Syne," over and over and then over again. Harper Faith, the fully perturbed waitress assigned to the men's table, felt on the verge of dousing the loud threesome with a pitcher of brew. She found the man with copper-colored hair particularly irksome; he irritated her even as he sat down at the table upon arriving at the diner two hours earlier when he said: "Sweetie" and then proceeded to pat her ample behind.

As the off-tune trio rounded out the song of remembrance, the copper haired man shouted for "Another pitcher, babe." Harper went to the host station, commiserated with the hostess by cussing and swearing until her face pulsed purple.

Harper Faith was most displeased with having to work the dinner shift on the holiday. But, she drew the short straw. Plus, of all the waiters and waitresses, she was the only one without children. Some of the others were married, some were divorced. Still others were single parents. But, to a person, they all had children at home for the holiday, except for Harper.

Upon drawing the wicked stick that led to her working on that night, Harper reasoned that the diner likely would not be all that busy as people would be engaged in holiday activities at home. Her assumption held true until the copper haired man and his cohorts arrived.

Her only other occupied station contained a solitary gentleman, a man Harper thought to be about seventy. He ordered a Porterhouse with a side of grilled onions and a glass of virgin egg nog.

Indeed, the older gent was so unobtrusive, Harper kept forgetting that he was there at all. Between being irked by the horribly out of tune and out of sync trio and generally miffed about drawing the short straw, Harper found herself losing track fairly frequently that evening.

49

Harper started to sneak off to the restaurant's rear delivery door, behind the kitchen, for a smoke break. Halfway to her desired destination, she stopped short realizing she had not popped by the kindly gent's table in some time. She hurried around back into the dining room. Reaching the man's post, she apologized for not being back to him sooner and asked if he needed anything.

"You know," he said in a voice that made Harper think what a wonderful grandfather he would be, kind
and loving, "I'll take another slug of this."

"Sure," Harper smiled, sincerely finding herself grinning. She took the man's glass and went back to the kitchen and poured him a fresh egg nog.

Returning to the man's table, she took a closer look at the chap. He did not look familiar to her, the restaurant having a goodly share of regulars. The man also looked tired, very tired and worn, to Harper.

"Are you from around here?" Harper asked.

The man looked as if he was on the brink of bursting into a gut-busting laugh.

"My, no," he said. "I'm actually from quite far off."

Harper imagined Peoria.

"Born and raised here," Harper volunteered about herself.

"I'm Nicholas." The old man struggled to stand as he introduced himself.

"Sit, sit. Don't get up for me," Harper extended her hand, shook his and gave him her name.

"Pleased to meet you," the old man graciously said.

"Same to you," she replied, thinking about a smoke once again. "You just let me know if you need anything else," she added, leaving the old man's table.

Harper retraced her steps back through the kitchen, on this occasion reaching the delivery door. She ducked outside, into the freezing Illinois winter night. She wasted no time in lighting up, finishing her smoke off in little time, not wanting to be out in the cold for too long.

Returning to the dining room, the loud trio was crashing through "Auld Lang Syne" for the umpteenth time. She rolled her eyes as the liquored up males once more butchered the lyrics.

"Go home," she muttered to herself. "Go away."

She glanced over at the old man, to see if the tragic rendition of "Auld Lang Syne" bothered him. He seemed well content, enjoying his egg nog and looking as if he were staring out the window and across the parking lot at the occasional car motoring down the roadway in front of the diner.

Harper thought about returning to the man's table to chat with him a bit further, but then thought better of it. He looked pleased enough to just be left alone and Harper did not want to bother him.

Just as she was about to turn away and walk back into the kitchen, the old man cocked his head and looked in the general direction of where Harper stood.

The old man's kindly glance compelled Harper to move in his direction.

"Are you doing okay?" she asked, finding herself smiling again.

"Oh, yes, I am," he responded emphatically.

Harper noticed he finished off his meal plate and that his egg nog was nearly gone.

"Would you like some dessert? We have great pie." He rubbed his hand on his chin, thinking.

"You know," he said, "I just had my beard shaved off this afternoon, so I'm not too used to actually feeling my chin."

He chuckled, a happy laugh.

Harper smiled, waited a moment, and then lightly prodded him further about dessert.

"You know," Harper said, putting her hands to her full hips, "the pie is on the house, this being a holiday and all."

Smiling all the while, he deliberately squeezed shut both his eyes as if to say 'How nice of you.'

51

"What kinds do you have?"

Harper rattled off the diner's fresh made, homestyle pie menu.

"Hmm," he replied, once more rubbing his fingers on his newly shorn chin. "How about a nice slice of blueberry?"

"My favorite," she honestly said. "Whipping cream?"

"Oh, please," he heartily replied as if Harper suggested something or another tremendously grand.

"Just like I like it," she added, leaving his table to fill his request.

She realized, on walking back to the kitchen, that the entire time she visited with the old man, she totally tuned out the noise rumbling from the three top table. She thought that she just might take a break and have a slice of blueberry pie herself; with the visitor if he did not mind the company of a waitress.

She found the diner's owner idling away in the kitchen and asked him if he objected to her taking a short break to have some dessert with one of her customers.

"It's a holiday after all," she remarked.

The owner agreed, noting: "Yeah, it's slow, too."

Harper put two slices of blueberry pie, warmed, with whipping cream on the side onto a serving tray. She filled up a couple of glasses of egg nog and then made her way back out to the dining room.

As expected, the drunken trio was well into "Auld Lang Syne," although Harper thought the song sounded more and more like "Camptown Races" as the night wore on and the men's singing ability degenerated further.

She walked up to the old visitor's table, placing one of the pie slices in front of him before she asked if he minded some company over dessert.

"That would be grand," he said, starting to stand in order to more gallantly extend Harper a seat.

"Sit, sit," she said, smiling at the comely gent.

Both the old man and Harper took pleasing first bites of the berry pie and whipping cream.

"Very good," he complimented.

"The pie here, it's always good," replied Harper.

"Very tasty," he reaffirmed.

"So," Harper continued. "You mentioned that you are from pretty far off ..." She allowed her voice to trail off, hoping to elicit some more information from him in order to move into smooth conversation.

"Yes, I am."

"I'm from here," Harper said with a shrug. "My whole life."

"Seems to be a nice town."

"I suppose." Harper spoke in the manner of all people who resided in the smaller towns of their birth into adulthood, a tone rife with resignation.

"Did you have a nice Christmas?" inquired the old visitor.

With another slump of her shoulders, Harper again said: "I suppose."

"You had to work," he stated the obvious.

Harper echoed: "I had to work." She added: "We drew straws to see who'd work."

He smiled and nodded as if he truly understood how Harper felt at that moment.

"I worked today myself," he remarked. Hearing that, Harper almost responded that he looked to be beyond his working years, but she caught herself.

"You and me," she ended up saying, identifying their commonality.

"You and me," he repeated, cutting off another bite of pie with his fork.

"Do you have children?' he asked. Something in his inflection, the rise and fall of his voice, made Harper wonder for a moment if he knew the answer to his question.

"No." Her face looked downcast when she spoke about not having a child.

"You're young," the old man said, desiring to buck

up his suddenly sagging table partner.

Harper nodded. She knew she was young, but she also understood the pratfalls and limitations of living in a small town. She also knew that she had not had a date with a fellow in a few years.

"You never know what the new year will bring."

The old visitor's tone was so encouraging she believed him, almost.

"So, will you be heading back home?" Harper asked, not having paid attention to the fact that Nicholas did not tell her where his home even was located.

"Oh, yes. Once I finish up here, I head back home."

"That'll be nice for you."

Harper looked more directly into the gentleman's eyes. She realized that old man's eyes were a color that she could only describe as being Christmas green.

"You have such pretty eyes," she remarked, speaking before she considered her words.

He flushed, his cheeks turning a bit rosy.

"Thank you, Miss Harper," he replied.

Fully engrossed in visiting with the old visitor, Harper did not at first hear the copper-haired, inebriated man at the three top table clamoring for another pitcher of beer. When she did finally catch the boisterous call for service, she politely and reluctantly excused herself from Nicholas.

Harper hurried and tapped a fresh pitcher, dropping it off with the loud threesome without even directly acknowledging them.

In barely a few minutes, she was reseated with the old man.

"Do you like the pie?"

"It's delicious," he replied.

"We have the best."

"You seem to," he agreed.

They did not speak for a couple of minutes while they each finished the pie slices.

"I end up traveling a good deal around Christmastime," the old man volunteered between sips of egg nog.

"Really?" asked Harper. "Why's that?"

He patted his lips with his napkin, then smiled. "My work," he softly explained.

"So, you're away from your family a lot at Christmas?" Harper asked.

"From my wife, I am."

"No children?"

"No children. Just my wife and me."

"What do you do?' Harper asked him.

"Shipping, I guess you'd say."

"I see," Harper said although she really did not.

He nodded, taking another swallow of egg nog. He eased back in his chair.

"You know, even though I find myself traveling at Christmastime, I always meet good people along the way, folks I never forget." "That would be nice."

He nodded in agreement.

"I remember a poor, young lad in Iowa, many years back. Back during the Depression ..." His voice trailed off, a smile still on his face.

Harper thought to herself: 'Boy, you are old if you were working way back in the 30s.'

"Uh – huh," she said, waiting to hear more of the old man's tale.

"Well, Miss Harper, I came to know this young fellow, probably about twelve or thirteen, 1 suppose." Harper nodded, taking some egg nog.

"He lived at his grandparents' house in a little Iowa town. He lived there with his father, who had been a farmer. But, because of the Depression, because of financial troubles, the farm was lost. They had to move into town to live with the grandparents." "Oh, how sad," Harper remarked.

"Yes, of course, losing the farm was rough. You see, Miss Harper, life was even tougher for those folks. The boy's mother had died not all that long before they lost the farm. Consumption is what they called it at the time, I think. Tuberculosis."

"Oh, dear," Harper sadly responded.

He carried on with his tale of the boy in Iowa.

"You see, Miss Harper, I would see this boy quite often sitting on a fence watching some ponies that were kept in a pasture not far from where he lived."

The old man took a generous slug of egg nog to refresh his throat. The break in his story, though minimal, was enough to allow for the sound of the raucous men at the other table to pierce Harper's concentration. They wanted another round.

Harper apologized to him, told her she would return "in a jiffy," and excused herself.

Snaring another fresh pitcher of brew, Harper reluctantly returned to the trio's table. Right after she set the new pitcher in front of the group, but before she could escape the table side, the man with the coppercolored hair reached out and wrapped his own arm around Harper's midsection.

"Hey babe," he blathered, "when 'ya gonna' sit with us, babe?"

Saying nothing, she yanked herself free of the groper and returned to the safety and comfort of the old man's table.

"I'm sorry," the old man said when she retook a seat at his table.

"For what?"

"For them," he explained.

"Oh, please," she chided. "They're not your fault." Pausing, she added: "Or my concern, for that matter."

Harper encouraged him to finish his story of the teenage boy in Iowa.

"Like I said," he went forth, "I saw this young lad regularly, watching these ponies in a pasture. Shetland ponies, as I recall. When I saw the boy, each time I saw the boy, he looked to be carrying the weight of the world on his shoulders."

Hearing that, Harper sighed.

"Turns out," he said, after acknowledging Harper's sympathetic sigh with a nod of his head and a blink of his Christmas green eyes, "turns out the sad looking lad had a younger brother and a younger sister. Twins." Harper's eyes echoed the sentiment of her sigh.

"The boy finally confided in me," the old man stated to Harper. "He finally told me there was no money to buy his little brother and sister Christmas gifts. Not a spare penny, Miss Harper."

Feeling for the boy, as the old man obviously still did as well, Harper shook her head.

"Miss Harper, you see I just could not let that be."

He went on to explain that he himself arranged for a pony to be delivered to the boy's home on that Christmas Day so long ago.

"And the best part, Miss Harper," he added with a brilliant twinkle in his eyes, "the very best part was that the pony was pregnant and had twin colts that very spring."

"A pony for each of them," Harper said.

"A pony for the boy and for his brother and sister."

Placing both of her hands on the tabletop palms down, Harper declared: "What a nice man you are."

The old man flushed red, as he had earlier, his cheeks each casting off a soft rosy glow.

"You would have done the very same," he told Harper.

They chatted on a while longer when he turned the discussion tables around to Harper's life.

"So, Miss Harper, tell me more about your life," he suggested. She realized she sounded trite, but nonetheless asked: "What's there to tell?"

Nonplussed, the old man said he imagined she could tell a good deal. "Well … like I said … I'm from here … originally."

"Yes."

"And I work here," she said, gesturing around the dining room with her right hand.

"Do you want some coffee?" she asked, intentionally trying to divert the conversation away from her and her life.

"No, thank you," he graciously declined. "But if you do …"

She shook her head. "Keeps me awake."

"Me, too." He chuckled. "You know, I have a long trip home to make yet tonight. So, on second thought, maybe I should have some."

"You do want some?" she asked.

"Let me wait and see. Tell me more about yourself, your life here."

"Well, let's see." Harper paused, trying to decide what to tell the man next. "I'm an only child. Both my folks have passed, going on four years for Ma, five for Pa."

She stopped speaking, in a manner that led the old man to conclude that the woman at his table finished with what she was willing to share.

Assuming she was single, Nicholas asked if she ever married.

Her expression slipped and he immediately regretted the question and wished he could stuff the words back into his mouth. Nevertheless, Harper answered after a moment and explained she had once, some twenty years back when she was just over eighteen.

"He left, for good, when I was pregnant …" Her voice trailed off.

"And the baby?" the old man asked with transparent hesitation.

"Adopted. I put him up. Thought it was best."

He wasted not a beat telling Harper that he was sure the child, her child, thought about her and wished her the best.

"Maybe so," she said, in an obviously doubtful tone.

58

"I'm certain," he said with a firmness that startled Harper.

Before she could say anything further, the restaurant's door opened and a young man walked in, wearing a stocking cap, hunter's plaid coat and carrying a knapsack on his back.

"A customer," she muttered, sounding disappointed because the arrival of the new patron would take her away from the old visitor.

"Will you be here for a bit longer?" she asked him.

He smiled and said: "A bit longer, yes."

Harper stood, went over to the young fellow and asked if he wanted to be seated in the smoking or nonsmoking section of the diner.

"Nonsmoking, please," he replied and looked as if he wanted to say something else. Harper waited for him to speak further and when he did not say anything more, she led him off to a table between the three top and Nicholas. She noticed that the threesome had stopped singing, for which she was relieved, grateful. But the men showed no sign of getting ready to depart, which made Harper moan, softly so as not to be overheard by her new customer.

Harper spent about ten minutes getting the young man settled in and his order taken and turned in to the solitary cook behind the grill. She also dropped a new, full pitcher off at the table of three men, wanting to get back to the old man and avoid having to deal with the dreaded copper-haired man for at least a while longer.

When she returned to the old man's table, he was finishing off the last of his egg nog.

"Would you like more?" she asked before retaking a chair.

"Oh, no, Miss Harper. But, you know, I will take that cup of coffee."

"Surely."

She retrieved fairly fresh cups of coffee for the both of them.

When she returned to the table, the old man mentioned to her that he frequently told the young lad in Iowa something that always seemed to cheer the boy up.

59

"What's that?"

"I used to tell the boy: 'Think the best thoughts and the best will come to you.'"

Harper smiled and told him that he spoke a nice sentiment and she would do her best to keep it in mind. Nicholas, saying nothing, nodded deeply while keeping his eyes closed. For a moment, Harper wondered if the old chap was checking into her own mind to see if she was thinking the best of thoughts.

Before either of them could speak any further, the man with the copper-colored hair called out for Harper, hollering for his group's tab. She felt relieved that they appeared to be ready to depart. Even if she had to endure another smack to her behind, which she surely hoped to avoid, she knew that they would be out the door in due course.

She wasted not a moment in getting the three top's bill settled. And she managed to dodge an incoming palm swipe aimed towards her rear end.

Right as she dispatched the obnoxious trio out the door and into the night, the solitary young man's order was up. Retrieving the meal, she went directly to his table.

"Here you go," she said, sounding more genuinely happy than she had all night. The conversation with the old visitor had brightened her spirits and lightened her mind. The three men departing helped even more.

"Can I ask you something?" the young man asked Harper. She assumed he wanted ketchup or some other condiment.

"Sure."

"Is your name Harper Faith?"

She thought nothing unusual about the query. Being in a small community, such a question was common. Harper thought she probably knew the young fellow's mother.

"Yes," she said, with a smile.

"My name's Mitch," he quickly responded. "Mitch Conley."

Harper engaged her memory, trying to place the Conley surname. She drew a blank. Before she asked if she was a friend of his folks, the young man said:

"This is hard."

Pausing, he inhaled deeply and continued.

"About nineteen years back, you had a baby. You had a baby boy."

The young man, Mitch, took in a second generous breath of air.

"Well, ma'am, that's me. I'm that baby, I'm that boy."

Neither Harper nor Mitch said another word for over a full minute. Indeed, Harper held her breath. Eventually, Harper turned around to see if Nicholas heard the conversation.

Much to her surprise, the old man was no longer seated at the table. Instead, she saw some cash piled next to his empty pie plate. Somehow the old visitor managed to depart the diner without her seeing him leave.

Not knowing what to say in response to Mitch, Harper nervously dashed over to the old man's table and fumbled around with the money he'd left behind.

On top of the cash for payment, he left a note that said: "*Harper,*

Think the very best thoughts and the very best will come to you.

Merry Christmas,

Nicholas."

Harper picked up the note, tears welling up in her eyes. She returned to Mitch's table, sitting down across from the young man. She spent the remainder of Christmas with Mitch, her child. She listened to his stories, tales of his life so far. When it came her turn to share with Mitch her own life's tale, she spoke first of an old man named Nicholas.

Umbrella Man

I wandered the long, winding rural road alone. The crisp April morning air was bracing and pleasant. Off to my right and off to my left, as far as I could see, were fields of green, inch high growth just pushing through the black Kansas soil.

The green expanse, from horizon to horizon, met with the rich blue of the early morning sky. Not a cloud, not a sprinkle of white, did I see anywhere.

I landed as the pastor of the small Catholic parish in Rossville, a small town nestled just west of the Kansas capital city of Topeka, two springs earlier in 1948. I hailed from a small Iowa berg, Otterville, and went from my boyhood home on a farm to Saint Meinrad's Seminary in Indiana then on to Saints Peter and Paul Catholic Church in Rossville.

Mondays, from the end of March until mid-October, I reserved for long early morning walks along the meandering dirt and pea gravel roads running away and around Rossville. The roads ran out of town like a dusty spider's web knitting through the green fields and pastures.

About an hour deep into my walk-about, I caught a glimpse of an unexpected dash of color different from the green and blue all around. I caught sight of a glorious glow a good hundred yards from my path on the roadway. Up next to a farmhouse, a rambling, white place with neatly trimmed green shutters that matched the hue of the encompassing fields and dales, was cut out a large garden plot.

Up and down over about a third of the garden patch was a burst of color – pinks and blues and violets and oranges. I squinted my eyes to try and get a better look, never having seen such a wild flush of blossoming blooms so early and so thick at that time of year.

In my two years in Rossville I came to know or at least know of most of the folks who lived in the area. But as I looked upon the busy, bursting strip of bright color, I realized that I did not know who owned that particular farm, who was responsible for planting and tending what looked like thick, healthy growth. I lost track of time, staring at the garden off in the distance. I did not hear the rack and rattle of the old Ford pickup truck making down the road, coming from the same direction that I had walked.

The rickety Ford slowed and stopped at the same time I paid attention to its appearance.

"Father White?" the driver, a sixty-something farmer, called out from the rusted cab.

I turned away from the garden patch for the first time since my discovery of the gaily growing blossoms.

"Hello, Warren," I greeted. I asked him at once who lived at the farm at which I was stopped.

Warren Rogers chuckled and shot me a look like I should know better. "It's those looney birds," Warren replied, looping a forefinger around his head.

"Those what?" I asked, having no idea what the good old fellow meant.

"Looney birds," he repeated, his finger still orbiting around his right ear. "Couple of looney birds, they is. That's who's livin' there … a couple real looney birds, that's what."

Warren finally rested his twirling hand, dropping it to his side.

Mustering a smile, not wanting to sound as if I was chiding Warren Rogers, I asked if he knew their names.

"Sure do," he proudly boasted, but said no more.

Keeping what I hoped was a pleasant, safe smile I asked: "And they are?" "What?" be asked.

"Their names," I replied.

"Who?" he asked, looking befuddled.

"The names of the people who own this farm." I pointed at the bright patch of color.

"Oh yeah, them looney birds. Not even sure if they're actually hitched up," Warren explained.

"Hitched?" I asked.

"Married … married up," Warren replied. "I'm not sure certain they'd even done got married up together to the other."

I nodded, still smiling. "So," I continued, "their names. What are their names?"

"Oh, sure," Warren responded. "They be Hester, she's the woman. Her father used to be a doctor some thirty years back, down the road in Topeka. He's gone now, 'course. Old Doc DeWayne. And the fellow who lives there … some fellow called Handy Weather. No idea where that fellow's come from. No idea at all."

"So, the people who live here are named Hester DeWayne and Handy Weather?" I asked.

Warren shook his head and said: "No." My smile slipped and I knew I looked hopelessly puzzled in spite of my best efforts.

"You lost me, Warren," I confided.

"You see," he replied. "Doc DeWayne's girl … that's Hester who lives here. She once got hitched up to a fellow named Therese, Richard Therese. He got himself killed sometime after they got married up … or so they says. But, no one ever come up with no body, you see. So I expect if Hester ain't married up to this Handy Weather fellow, she's still to be called Hester Therese."

"You're probably right," I acknowledged, my smile returning as my confusion passed.

"Need a ride somewhere, Father White?" Warren asked.

"I'm just out for a walk. But, thanks," I told the old farmer.

"A walk?" Warren asked me like I told him I was planning an outer space trip to the moon.

"Right." I smiled.

"Whad' ya' mean? A walk?"

"I'm just out for a walk, that's all," I replied.

"But where ya goin'?" he asked.

"Nowhere special. Just out for a walk."

At that remark, Warren Rogers looked at me with the same expression he used when he described the owners of the house with the peculiar garden plot as being "looney birds." I thought I needed to accept a ride from Warren to avoid having the farmer say about me: "Father Al White? I reckon he's a looney bird. Just wanders around, going nowhere at all."

But, I decided to risk it and bid the skeptical farmer a good day and continued my walk down the road.

I returned to the rectory house, directly next to the church, in time for lunch. The parish housekeeper, a plump, Berlin-born woman of sixty who'd served the parish's pastors for forty years, had a hearty lunch prepared and waiting for me upon my return. As was our custom, except on Sundays, Hilda joined me for the noon meal.

Having been in the United States for over four decades, on the plains of Kansas where speech was as flat as the prairie, Hilda's voice bore only a trace of her Germanic birth.

As we ate, I mentioned coming upon the house with the odd, early blossoms.

"It was strange," I said in summation of my morning trek. Hilda chuckled.

"What?" I asked, imagining she chortled at my rambling, weekly morning walks, as she did from time to time.

"Strange?" she asked, still alight with laughter.

"I didn't get close, but the patch was already blooming. All colors. Pink. Red. Orange. Purple." "You said 'strange'?" I nodded.

"The people or the flowers?" She laughed again, at what was a joke she alone understood at the moment.

"Meaning?"

"The people ... who live there." Hilda mimicked the twirling finger I saw earlier that day, performed by Warren Rogers. "Yonky-bonky," she said.

I chuckled myself at her terminology. "Yonkybonky?" I asked.

65

"Those people, at the house you saw."

"Yonky-bonky?"

"Crazy," she clarified.

"That's what Warren Rogers told me." "Warren Rogers?" she asked.

Between bites of Hilda's tender pot roast I explained that I saw the old farmer that morning while walking about.

"Oh, Father, I don't mean to be foul-mouthed. But old Hester and that Handy ... They're quite a crazy pair."

I smiled and teased my housekeeper with the prospect of her walking across the lawn to the church for confession.

"Really ... I don't mean any harm. Really, I don't."

Although I was more and more intrigued about hearing more of Hester, Handy and the garden patch, I knew Hilda baked a German apple pie that morning.

"Know what?" I said, shifting gears.

"What, Father?"

"I can still smell the pie you baked."

"Whipping cream?" she asked, adding: "It's fresh."

"On the side."

In a couple of minutes Hilda served up triangular slabs of still warm pie with healthy scoops of whipping cream to the side.

When Hilda and I nearly finished our pie slices, she reminded me of an appointment I had that afternoon with a young man from town, a dentist who settled in Rossville and hung a shingle at about the same time of my own arrival. I excused myself, telling Hilda I would be in my study.

"Just bring him back," I instructed, referring to my appointment.

I settled in behind my desk, which belonged to my father, a piece of furniture that stood at the edge of my family's parlor in our farmhouse in Otterville when I was a boy. When my father passed in '49, Mom thought I might like the desk. With great effort, I managed to get the desk from Northeast Iowa to Northeast Kansas, glad I arranged for the move.

66

In the very left corner of the aged desktop was an indentation of perhaps half an inch – a smooth, worn spot. My father had one nervous habit, a tic so constant that the gentle curve down in the wood at the corner was created.

I can rarely remember a time when my father was posted at his desk that he did not clutch the corner of the desk, rubbing his thumb on the top. Slowly, very slowly, he wore the groove.

Since the desk arrived in the study at Saints Peter and Paul Catholic Church rectory, I had developed my own habit whenever I sat at the desk of resting my thumb in the niche created by my father.

Eventually, after taking to my study, Hilda poked her head through the open door and announced the arrival of my afternoon appointment, the young dentist. A regular Sunday church-goer, combined with two visits of my own to his professional chair, I felt pretty familiar with the fellow. When he arrived at the rectory study that Monday in March, I immediately noticed that the young dentist did not look exactly well; he did not look quite right.

The man's hair was disheveled, his face ashen like dust from burnt coal pieces. He looked oddly unfamiliar to me despite my knowing the man rather well. At the instant, I even forgot his name. I frowned, not wanting to say "What happened to you?" Let alone "What in the world is your name?" I managed: "Tea. Let me fetch us some tea."

I motioned to the chair in front of my father's desk and made a quick exit from the study. I retreated to the kitchen, finding Hilda chopping carrots for supper.

"Hilda," I said, entering the room, "he doesn't look well at all."

"Not at all," she agreed.

"Hilda, I forgot his name. I know it as well as mine. But, what is it?"

Grinning, with a spray of mischief, my housekeeper responded: "Yours or his?

I laughed, a bit. "Hilda …"

67

"It is Dr Rydel," she began, when I interrupted with: "Clinton?"

"Clinton Rydel," she confirmed.

I started from the kitchen, stopping short just at the door. "Tea, Hilda. Do you have some tea?" "Hot or iced?" she asked.

"Either."

"Iced, yes. Hot, Father, I'd need to brew."

"Iced, then."

Without a pause, Hilda prepared a serving tray with a pitcher of tea and two glasses. Armed with the beverages, I returned to the study.

Somehow in my brief absence Clinton Rydel managed to look even grayer, his hair more messed as if he pulled at his head. Depending on what was on his mind, I imagined hair yanking might be a possible response. He seemed to crumble before my eyes, like a nearly spent chunk of furnace coal.

I did not bother pouring glasses of tea, figuring that if Clinton Rydel wanted refreshment he would pour on his own accord. Armed with his name, my memory itself refreshed, I felt it best to carry on with the appointment without an obvious interruption for drink service.

"Well, Dr Rydel ... Clinton ... how have you been?"

"Father, can I ask you something?"

His voice sounded surprisingly strong considering his outward appearance, his speech most direct. However, he looked to the floor and not at me when he spoke, all the while kneading his hands.

I rested my own hands on the desk, my thumb naturally sliding into my father's groove. "Of course." I nodded in what I hoped to be a reassuring fashion. "This isn't confession, though, right?" "What do you mean?" I asked.

"Well, Father, I know in confession, what I say is private ... secret."

"I see," I replied. "Consider what you say here today the same. Private. Secret. Between us."

He slowly nodded, still looking at the floor but somehow seeming to be weighing my words, my promise of confidentiality.

"Father, you know my wife ..." His voice trailed off leaving me uncertain as to whether he expected a response from me at the moment. I nodded, but realized he still was not looking at me, his face averted downward.

"Yes, of course. Mary Kay."

I found no problem recalling her name, unlike my earlier difficulties with her husband's moniker.

He nodded after I spoke his wife's name and then continued. "We've been married for five years."

"I didn't know that," I replied, more to fill what became an uncomfortable and soundless gap in the conversation.

"We're from Virginia, you know."

I did not, or at least did not recall, that geographic detail. I said "Uh-huh" nonetheless.

"Well, I'm from Virginia, I mean. She's from ... my wife's from Topeka, from right here in Kansas."

"Yes," I finally said, filling another awkward break.

"We met in Virginia Beach."

"I see."

"Got married. I came here. She wanted to live near her family and all that."

"I see."

"They needed a dentist here in Rossville. So it all worked out pretty well, I suppose."

"Yes, I suppose so."

Clinton Rydel carried on for a quarter of an hour, prancing about details relating to his wedding and move to Kansas and early life with Mary Kay, his wife. His eyes never left the floor and then he said: "I killed her, Mary Kay."

I gripped onto my desk so hard that a part of me actually was surprised that I did not poke through my father's worn spot with my thumb. I nearly gasped, but did not and not because of self control. Rather, my lungs, indeed my entire body, felt frozen. I could not move. I did not speak and probably could not have even if I was determined to do so.

"I did," Clinton eventually muttered, speaking as if his stony announcement of homicide required verbal confirmation.

Finally, words began to form, at least within the confines of my own head:

"When? Where? Why? How?" I thought. I knew the answer to "what" at that juncture, obviously. Despite appreciating that one of perhaps another of these possible single word queries was better placed, more appropriate that the others, the first that tumbled from my mouth happened to be the least acceptable, I imagined.

"How?" I asked.

I regretted the question the moment the lonely syllable slipped from my lips.

"Gun," Clinton replied.

"When?"

"This morning."

"Where?"

"At home," he responded, adding: "I called in sick to the office."

"Why, Clinton? Why?"

With that asked, the homicidal dentist finally removed his gaze from the floor.

"Father, she deserved it."

Although I thought the "what" question was answered with the knowledge that Mary Kay Rydel was killed by her husband, I asked "What?" instinctively to Clinton's matter-of-fact reply to my question of why. Speaking louder, almost as if he thought I did not hear well, Clinton repeated: "She deserved it, Mary Kay did."

Aghast, I asked: "What in the world do you mean?"

70

Clinton furrowed his brow and tossed my question back at me, speaking in what seemed a close to flippant tone. "What do you mean?"

"How in God's name could Mary Kay ... your wife, Clinton ... how could she deserve to be shot ... by you?"

I half expected the thus far casual and cool sounding fellow to shrug his shoulders and say: "Gosh, priest-man, beats me. Beats me."

He said only: "She just did." The three words fell like cats-eye marbles onto a wooden floor.

I felt a tightening in my stomach. My immediate desire was to push my father's desk out of the room, away from this man. I felt that the presence of Clinton Rydel defiled the old desk, my father's memory.

I wanted Clinton Rydel gone. I wanted to take a long, hot shower. I wanted to be a boy back home in Otterville, Iowa. And, at that precise moment, I shuddered, I obviously shuddered. My brain flashed a long buried memory from back when I was just a boy, gleaning a corn field at harvest time.

Two of my childhood friends and I stumbled upon a body, a dead boy's body, in a little patch of woods near the field in which we scooped together errant ears of corn. I felt my gut tighten, knot up horribly.

"You need confession," I managed to say, grimly.

Clinton did not move, his pale green eyes looked into my own. I broke the stare, turning my own gaze to the worn spot on my desk top. "And you have to go to the Sheriff."

Clinton jumped to his feet, his face flushed red before he was fully standing. "You said you could not tell anyone anything I said!"

I did not know whether I should stand or continue sitting.

I definitely worried about what a man who killed his wife was capable of doing to another person to whom he was never wed. Certainly, in my mind, it was not beyond the realm of possibility for such a man to turn on his parish priest and unsuspecting housekeeper.

71

"Calm down," I retorted, a surprising amount of authority in my voice. "I can't tell anyone what you've told me, that's true. And I won't. But you … you need to – you have to go to the Sheriff."

"I do not!" Clinton shouted and I was certain he was heard by Hilda off in the kitchen. Under the circumstances, I hoped she would stay put and not wander back to see what developed in my study. How I would explain the situation to a curious Hilda I certainly could not imagine.

"Clinton, try and calm down," I said, having no idea what else to say or do with the crimson faced dentistturned-murderer hovering at my desk flexing his fingers in and out, forming fists and releasing. I realized saying anything further about the Sheriff at that time would be pointless, counter productive, perhaps even dangerous.

"Do you want confession?" I asked.

"I don't know," he replied, using the same harsh, nearly fierce inflection. He repeated "I don't know," the second time, his tone a notch lower but far from calm.

"I think you should," I stated with all of the certainty I could muster on the moment.

Over the course of the next quarter of an hour, Clinton Rydel and I fully reached an impasse. I gained only one concession; an assurance from Clinton Rydel that he would return to see me at the rectory after supper. I hoped giving him some time to consider his situation and his murdered wife would result in Clinton reaching the decision to face the Sheriff at the Courthouse and his maker at the Church. But, I had no illusions about the dentist actually reappearing at the rectory.

I ushered Clinton out the front door, wondering of the propriety of freely bidding adieu to a self-declared wife killer. After shutting the dentist out of the rectory I made my way to the kitchen to see what Hilda had or perchance had not heard of my visit. I entered the kitchen as the housekeeper finished putting up the lunch dishes.

"So?" I asked upon walking through the door into the room.

"Doc Rydel gone?" she returned, not turning from the cabinet at which she struggled to return a serving platter to the top shelf. Her back turned to me, I could not make out her expression. However, the unemotional tenor of her voice led me to conclude she heard nothing of importance. On some level, I wished Hilda had heard all. I badly wanted to talk.

"Need help?" I asked, regarding the platter exactly at the moment she managed to get it into place.

"Got it." She turned around and belied no expression that suggested she heard the discussion in the study.

At that moment, I found myself terribly torn. I had met with a murderous parishioner that I sent on his own way. I wanted to unbridle myself with the housekeeper, but my vows prevented me from gut spilling, from human contact. On the whim I announced: "I'm going for a walk."

"Again?" she asked, surprised.

I nodded, turned and exited the room, uncertain as to whether I could dutifully survive further questioning without slipping and spilling the secrets of my study.

Never before having taken to the lonely rural roads around Rossville after noon, I immediately was stunned at how very different the scene looked in the glow of the westerly sun. Places I had only before seen veiled in shadow were beautifully lit with the soft rays of spring, other spots that shone brilliantly in the morning light seemed all but gone.

Despite the pretty afternoon, and a near perfect temperature, the visit from Clinton Rydel remained well affixed at the tip of my thoughts. Death was commonplace enough of an occurrence in my profession, an integral part of my vocation. But murderous dentists who slay wives seemed unique. Only one other fellow in my seminary class had faced a confession of homicide since our ordination, that I knew of at least. And his case involved a man who clubbed another man with a table leg in a riotous bar brawl, not a husband against his very own wife.

Although I was not conscious of setting a true course for my irregular afternoon stroll, I ended up for the second time that day standing on the road in front of the peculiar patch of early bloomers, in front of the farm that belonged to the apparently uneven folk called Handy and Hester.

Gazing upon the pastel colors of the garden patch, I quickly realized that it looked different from how it had appeared just that very morning. Immediately, I chalked the changed appearance to the different slant of the sun. But shortly I determined the alteration in the patch was not merely the illusory workings of bright light and veiling shadow.

Standing roadside and looking across the green pasture over to the farmhouse and on to the garden, I thought with near certainty that the flower patch had grown, grown wider. There appeared to me to be even more rows of pinks and blues and violets and oranges. What in the morning appeared to cover no more than a third of the garden seemed to have spread to over half the plot. Mysterious blossoms magically spreading, I thought. I wondered, for the moment, whether if I stood very still I might witness new, pretty colored blossoms open over the garden patch, bettering the glorious carpet of spectacular hues right before my eyes.

I lost track of time, just as in the morning.

And, somehow and someway, thoughts of Clinton Rydel and his unnecessarily deceased wife slipped away. I toyed with the idea of walking across the pasture and over to the farmhouse and the brilliant blooms, to pick a flower or two. But, just as I was about to make across the tender spring alfalfa that grew inch high in the pasture, the door to the house swung open and out walked a thin man, who looked to be middleaged or perhaps just a tad more. He did not seem to notice my presence.

I watched the man, secure at my distance in knowing I could merely begin walking down the road again should he glance my way and he would be none the wiser about my gazing at his beautiful flower patch. He would not know that I gaped and gawked at the pretty creation next to his house.

I assumed the man to be Handy Weather, of offbeat character and unbalanced nature according to the old farmer and my faithful housekeeper.

The fellow, Handy, strutted over to the garden patch, hoisting up his britches as he walked. He likewise scratched himself most indelicately, a sure sign – or so I believed – that he knew not of my nearby presence and directed gaze.

At the garden's edge, Handy plopped down to his knees and quickly bent over further still. From my vantage point on the road, the odd fellow appeared to be looking under the brilliantly bright blooms, to be peering under the glorious and queer flower buds of the early season.

The words of Warren Rogers, the farmer, quickened in my thoughts: "Those looney birds." The comments of Hilda reverberated as well – "Yonky-bonky."

I thought, in spite of myself: 'Oh, yonky-bonky looney bird, how doth thy garden grow?'

As if in some sort of sudden retribution that caught me so off guard, I nearly tripped to my knees when the fellow at the garden, that Handy Weather, bellowed at the tip top of his lungs: "Hester!"

He shouted again: "Hester!" His voice bore a youthful eagerness. Simply put, his was a happy voice.

Once more the door to the house opened and out trundled a stout woman who managed lumbering steps. Reaching the garden patch, with great effort she joined Handy on her knees next to the flowerbed. She too crouched further and appeared to be looking underneath the blooms.

A guilty rush invaded me not long after the woman joined the man. I felt as if I wormed into something special, something private, by peeking at the doings of Hester and Handy from the dirt road. Flooded by such feelings, I hurried home.

The closer I drew to the rectory, the more a dreadful feeling of gloom stifled my senses. Clinton Rydel and his murdered wife, a most hard and harsh reality, returned full force to my thoughts, quite like the mad rush of freezing water from a well-primed pump.

I returned to my study without so much as a "hello" to Hilda in the kitchen. Faced with the prospect of another possible and at least planned visit from Doc Rydel, I knew the remainder of the afternoon would grind miserably slowly.

My thoughts became jumbled fare, mixed images of Clinton Rydel and the blooming garden patch, of an Iowa cornfield and a dead boy's body so many years earlier, all mingled and meshed. The horrors that life can bring blended with the beauty that living can many times bear.

I slid my thumb onto the worn spot on my father's desk and with my other hand began making a round of my rosary beads. I was halfway through the circuit of "Our Father's" and, mostly, "Hail Mary's" when Hilda entered the room.

"Father?" she softly said, obviously not wanting to disturb me. I looked up.

"Father," she continued nervously, once gaining my attention. "Sheriff Menely … he's here."

"Here?" I asked, knowing the man, but also knowing him to be a Lutheran.

"Here."

"Now?" "Now."

"Oh," I said.

I naturally imagined the visit was related to Clinton Rydel and asked: "Troubles?"

Hilda nodded, wiping her dry hands on her apron, a nervous habit.

"Yes, then," I replied. "Well, bring him in, then."

She nodded, hurried away, and in a moment returned with the Sheriff at her heels.

I stood, greeted the lawman and offered him a seat. He was tall, prematurely graying and tan despite the early time of year.

"How are you?" I asked.

"Oh, no complaints," he replied in a voice that seemed tinged with the round accent of the Ozark Mountains some four hours southeast of Rossville. Hilda managed to vanish, rather like a magician's assistant stashed in a tricky box.

"Seems this isn't a social call ..." I suggested.

"Oh ... no," he replied, nonplussed.

"How might I help you?" I cleared my throat.

"You know of Tim Fellows?" he asked.

A parishioner, so I nodded.

"An' his wife, Rita?"

"Louise."

"Louise?"

"Louise."

"Oh," he replied, pulling a tiny notebook from the breast pocket of his navy blue uniform shirt. He scribbled a note.

"Mrs Fellows, she tells me you may have seen Doc Rydel today ..."

I sat still. I recollected that the Fellows lived next door to the Rydels.

"Seems ole Doc Rydel, seems he told ole Mrs Fellows he was headin' here to see you." I did not move.

"Anyways, like it is, of Doc Rydel ... looks like he done an' gone shot up of Mrs Rydel. Just this mornin'. An' now he's gone a-missin'. But Mrs Fellows says she heard the commotion over to the Rydels. She was out waterin' her 'tunia plants, I guess. Ole Doc Rydel comes outta his house and tells of Mrs Fellows he's comin' on down to see you. Says it after Mrs Fellows asks about the commotion and all." "Oh," I managed.

"Course, Mrs Fellows, she telephoned us up, reportin' the commotion and all."

"Oh."

We sat in silence for what seemed a full season on the Church's calendar. Sheriff Menely finally spoke. "So, you seen him or what?"

"Clinton Rydel?" I asked, buying a slip of time to think.

"Yep."

"Yes." "You did then?" I

nodded. "This mornin'?"

I nodded.

"Here?"

I nodded.

"Know where he's gone off to?" I shook my

head, honestly.

The Sheriff rose, seeming satisfied with what he obtained from me, a surprise in my mind. I imagined a long interrogation, me continually invoking the privilege of the confessional, a scene from a John Ford motion picture.

"You know," Sheriff Menely boasted, "I've been to them training sessions off in Kansas City. I know all

'bout that priest and convict confession thing."

In spite of myself I slivered off a grin at the Sheriff's quick move to place Clinton Rydel in convict status.

I rose and replied: "Of course. I knew you would have."

"Can you telephone me if you see him?"

"I suppose I can. I'd tell him I was doing it though."

"Seems fair enough."

I walked the Sheriff to the front door of the rectory, neither of us speaking. In the foyer, just before he departed, Sheriff Menely remarked: "Sad business."

"Yes."

"He's the only dentist we done got."

With the Sheriff gone, I walked back to the study and settled in behind my desk to finish the rosary. Once more, Hilda was at the door to the room. "Father?" Her voice was soft.

78

"Hilda, yes?"

"Father … Gwen Mersh … she's here."

"Who?"

Hilda apologized and explained that Gwen Mersh was the late Mary Kay Rydel's sister from Topeka. "Oh Lord," I muttered. "Will you want tea?" I shrugged, myself at a loss.

"I'll get her," Hilda advised.

I stood up from my chair and remained standing until Gwen Mersh entered.

"Hya Father." The woman, looking to be in her midthirties, had a peculiarly chipper voice, I thought. Except for red rimmed eyes, tell-tale signs of crying, she appeared perfectly at ease, strangely composed and oddly content. "May I?" she asked, pointing at a chair in front of the desk.

"Please."

She propped a huge, shiny black leather handbag on her lap. She was a trim woman in a powder blue suit with large, oversized brass buttons in the shape of anchors. Her chestnut brown hair was pulled back in a most efficient bun.

"I'm Gwen Mersh," she introduced, looking dead on into my eyes, firm and unblinking. I introduced myself.

"So good to meet ya."

"Tea? Would you like some tea?"

She seemed to consider my offer of refreshment for a moment and then declined.

"I expect you've heard?"

I grimaced reflexively and slightly nodded with my eyes closed.

"Oh, yes, my sister … she's done got herself murdered."

At the strident remark, my eyes popped open, just as Gwen Mersh reached into her handbag.

"I've made lists …" she continued with the same efficiency she must have used in styling her hairdo. She pulled what looked to be a half dozen sheets of paper from the large purse. Setting the

79

handbag on the floor she rested the sheets on her lap, plucking one off the top of the stack, setting it on my desk.

"Obituary. Wrote it myself. Can you see the newspaper gets it? I don't mention Mary Kay going and getting herself murdered, of course."

Before I could respond, perhaps comment on the concept of Mary Kay Rydel "going and getting herself murdered," Gwen Mersh was on page two with all the sure swiftness of Mr Paul Harvey. In fact, she said: "Page two."

"List of ushers, altar boys. Can you get a copy of this over to Brennan's Funeral Home? They'll handle things, of course."

Even though Gwen Mersh appeared to be paying little attention to me, I made an effort to nod my head. I knew people handled grief differently. But, Gwen Mersh marked the first occasion in which I confronted a person seeming to deal with grief with efficiency.

"Songs," she said, laying page number three upon my desk. She smiled and added almost coquettishly:
"I'll do the solos, of course." "Of course,"

I muttered.

Plopping page four on my desk, she explained that the paper contained a list of suggested Bible readings for the funeral Mass.

"Okay." I barely managed a whisper.

Gwen Mersh ended up placing a few more sheets of paper in front of me, briefly explaining each in turn. When finished, she collected her handbag, rose to her feet and brightly advised: "I'm off to Brennan's. Need to pick out a casket, don't ya know."

And with that Gwen Mersh was out the door, showing herself the way out of the rectory.

Picking up my rosary to finish my prayers, the telephone clanged to life.

"Hello?" I greeted.

"Father?"

"Yes?"

"Sheriff Menely here. Hey, we done got ahold of Doc Rydel. We done arrested the fellow." "I see."

"So then, just wanted to let you know and all after our meetin'. One of my deputies done snatched the Doc while you an' me was a-meetin'."

"I see." Taking a deep breath I then asked if Clinton Rydel mentioned wanting to see a priest, to see me.

"No he ain't done nothin' like that."

"Thank you, Sheriff."

I disconnected the call and, as if on cue, Hilda entered the study with iced tea and fresh, frosted sugar cookies. She brought a glass along for herself and took the chair occupied by Gwen Mersh only a few minutes earlier.

"A long day, Father?"

"Do you know what happened?"

She blushed and admitted to hearing some of what Clinton Rydel had all but shouted that morning. "And, of course, Gwen Mersh told me on the stoop the second I opened the door that she was here to see you because her sister's 'done and gone got herself killed.' I guess she actually said 'got herself murdered'."

"Clinton needs confession."

"He'll call for you, Father."

"You think?"

"I do."

We finished our glasses of chilled tea and ate the still warm from the oven cookies, speaking very little.

The next couple of days passed in a flurry, the township all abuzz with the news of Mary Kay Rydel's murder, Doc Rydel's arrest and the victim's efficiently arranged funeral at Saints Peter and Paul Church, my parish.

The funeral Mass, held on Thursday morning, brought a packed church. Gwen Mersh commanded the memorial service like a stockade matron and sang the 'Ave Maria' at the end with efficiency and no seeming regard for musical niceties.

On Friday Sheriff Menely relayed a message to me from Clinton Rydel; the dentist sought confession. I obliged in haste, worried all week that Clinton Rydel would face his maker by some fluke of dire fate before he took occasion to address his state of mortal sin.

Never having to take the confession of a self proclaimed killer, I was nervous, anxious. Hilda drove me to Topeka, some ten miles east, to the county lockup. She volunteered to drive as she was convinced that in my distracted state I would poorly navigate the paved although winding road to the government seat.

Arriving at the jail on Friday morning, the guards on duty quickly arranged for my session with Clinton Rydel. In the absence of a confessional, Clinton decided that he preferred our chairs to be set back to back so that he would not have to look at me, and me at him, while he confessed to the sin he previously told me about face to face.

Had I not known what was coming next, considering the tone of the initial words Clinton Rydel uttered in his confession, I would have thought I was about to hear the naughty disclosures of a teenaged boy or another such minor league n'er do well.

"Bless me father, for I have sinned ..." the dentist began in a sort of sing-song voice. "I made my last confession about one month ago."

He paused at that point as if expecting an accolade from me for being a regular recipient of the Sacrament.
I sat quietly.

"My greatest faults are ..."

As he continued, I found myself gripping the edge of the seat of my chair tightly with both hands, my knuckles white from the intensity.

The dentist carried on: "I took the Lord's name in vain ..."

I released a hand and scratched my head, not expecting heavenly cursing to be the first transgression out of Clinton

Rydel's mouth. Nevertheless, I thought of the penance I usually assigned to that sin; the Hail Mary, four times.

And, at that instant, I broke into a cold sweat. 'Thank God, literally,' I thought. 'Thank God that we are not sitting face to face.' I realized I had no idea what penance to give to a man who murdered his wife. I immediately became so wrapped up in that point, I paid little attention to Clinton Rydel's litany of venial sinning.

I forced myself to redirect my attention to what the dentist was saying after almost a minute passed. If nothing else, Clinton Rydel was a thorough confessor, or so it seemed.

"And I had lustful thoughts about Roxie Spish ..."

Not a parishioner, so I did not form a visual image.

"I swiped a newspaper, a Topeka Capital, off a table at Peg's Dinette ..."

Peg's Dinette, I reflected, great chicken fried steak sandwiches.

"And, oh yeah, I shot Mary Kay."

The words echoed in my head: *"And, oh yeah, I shot Mary Kay."*

The words sounded in tone and cadence like he said: "And, oh yeah, I fibbed on my time card at the plant."

Or: "And, oh yeah, I fiddled with my privates."

Not: "I shot and killed my wife."

I responded: "Well ..."

He said: "Yeah?"

Clinton sounded impatient, as if he expected me to say: "Well, Doc, thanks for the swell confession. For your penance, light a candle and say a Hail Mary."

I must have sat quietly for longer than I realized because Clinton, sounding irritated, said: "Father, can we get on with this?"

"Right," I said with no penance coming to mind.

"Well, then, Clinton ... are you sorry for your sins?"

"Yeah."

'Yeah …' I thought, parroting the penitent to myself. "Well, you know this is serious?" I asked.

"You mean the part about Mary Kay?"

Dumbfounded with his placid sounding statement of the most obvious, I snapped back: "Well, of course that part about Mary Kay."

"Yeah … that …" he replied.

"Say one thousand Hail Marys," I blurted, the words tumbling almost uncontrollably from my mouth.

"Say what?"

"The Hail Mary … one thousand times."

"One thousand times?"

Firmly, I advised that saying the Hail Mary a thousand times was a fair trade off as a penance for wife killing.

"All at once," he asked, as if negotiating the price of sheep.

"Finish in two days."

Personally not wanting to, I nonetheless gave the man absolution. I hurried from the jailhouse, prodded Hilda to best the speed limit on the way back to the rectory and, upon arriving, dashed to the bathroom upstairs next to my bedroom. After vomiting, I drew a hot bath and soaked in the tub for over an hour. On my own, I said one hundred Hail Marys.

After the respite in the soothing water, I redressed and went downstairs, joining Hilda in the kitchen for lunch.

"Are you okay?" she asked.

"It was hard." She nodded.

"Has this happened before? Here?" I asked.

"One time, a dozen years ago." "A
parishioner killed someone?" She nodded.

"What happened? Who?"

"Oh, they're gone now." Her face flushed. "I mean, the whole family's gone. The husband dead. The wife shot the husband. A shooting, just like with the Rydels."

"I see."

84

"Father Rice, he was the pastor here then. He had a hard time with it, just like you. A hard time with the whole mess."

"I'm sure."

Hilda spent a bit more time filling in a smattering of other details relating to the prior incident of intra-family homicide. When she finished, she suggested I take a walk.

"But it's not Monday," I responded, referring to my normal strolling day.

"Oh, be untamed Father," she smiled.

"You know, Hilda, a walk sounds like just the right thing for me."

"Off you go, then."

Leaving the rectory, I guessed the temperature out of doors to be somewhere in the seventies that Friday afternoon. The sky was a deep blue with a scattering of small and fluffy white cloud puffs. The little clouds looked quite like young lambs flirting about in a mellow pasture.

The sun had just slid over to the western half of the sky, bright, golden and reassuring.

I wondered if I had become something of an automaton because I ended up back square in front of the farmstead that was the home of the allegedly peculiar couple of Handy Weather and Hester Therese. On the occasion of my third visit, I knew absolutely that the colorful blossoms of the garden patch had spread even further, covering nearly all of the tended area.

As I looked upon the ever spreading blooms, Hester and Handy walked into my view from the backside of the farmhouse. On this occasion, they caught sight of me and each waved in friendly fashion. I did the same and then decided to walk across the trim alfalfa pasture towards the house, the couple and the garden.

Wearing my Roman collar, which I forgot to remove after my visit to the jailhouse, Handy and Hester easily identified me both as a Catholic priest and as the local pastor, Rossville being a small town.

85

"Hello, Father." Handy spoke first, Hester immediately repeating the hospitable greeting.

"Hello there."

Reaching the yard and standing only a few yards from the garden, my eyes were diverted from the faces of the welcoming hosts to the brilliant patch of color that had engaged my attention and regularly invaded my thoughts for days. Before I really could think, the words slipped from my mouth.

"What in the world?" I exclaimed.

Both Hester and Handy beamed proudly, like pleased parents.

I squeezed my eyes shut not one but three times, trying to adjust to what actually lay in front of where I stood, the gaily colored garden patch.

Clearly noticing my incredulous expression, Handy spoke. "You know, Father, Hester was married once before and her husband came up with these. He was an inventor, of sorts, I expect you could say. He invented these."

Handy broadly gestured with his right hand, a sweeping movement over the garden patch.

"He did," Hester confirmed.

Before me lay not a bed of unusually early blooming flowers. Rather, a clutter of what looked like tiny umbrellas covered nearly the entire expanse. Dainty parasols of thin paper on slender sticks poked into the garden's soil.

"Umbrellas?" I asked, confused and yet delighted by the scene.

"Oh, yes," Handy replied. Hester, smiling broadly, nodded along. "Made of paper."

"But why?"

"Oh, silly," Hester rejoined. "To block the sun." "Block the sun?" I was puzzled.

"Oh, yes," Handy replied once more. "This is our cabbage patch."

"And our cabbages are just sprouts," Hester interjected.

"Sprouts," Handy agreed. "And we don't want them to get scorched … scorched by the sun, don't you know."

"That's right," Hester affirmed.

"So little paper umbrellas …" I remarked.

"That's what Hester's husband … well, her long ago husband … that's what he invented," explained Handy.

"To cover the cabbage sprouts, to keep them safe," Hester remarked.

I spent the next few hours with Hester and Handy, sitting beside their cabbage patch. I listened to their stories. How they met, where they met. I heard about Hester's sad past, losing her first husband and her child in such a strange way and it brought me back for a moment to the evil in the world and the sad couple whose fate had made me want to escape for a walk that day. Hester and Handy both spoke of the famous actress that brought them together and they still praised her and mourned her passing.

As they reminisced, I thought about the colors in the garden, and the shades of gray in life itself. People thought this couple crazy and further proof of it was before my eyes in those little, colorful umbrellas protecting those cabbage sprouts. But what was truly crazy or evil was a man killing his wife in cold blood. To all the world my penitent and his wife looked perfectly sane until their awful tragedy became the source of town gossip and hit the papers across the state.

I felt a sense of peace knowing that there remained a place in the world where a man loved a woman, where a woman loved a man, and where little cabbage sprouts were kept safe beneath paper umbrellas. If this was crazy, then perhaps I was crazy too.

Miss Trent Plays the Jayhawk

Christmas Eve.

Pam Ella Trent breezed into the ornate lobby of the Hotel Savoy in downtown Kansas City, Missouri at noon on the dot. She planned her appearance to coincide with the rush and bustle of luncheon diners who made their treks through the lobby at that time en route to the hotel's elegant eatery. Scribbling her signature on napkins, scraps of paper, and porter cards, Miss Trent received her fans, women and men, who recognized her instantly.

Spending nearly half an hour wrapped in the glow of her admirers, Miss Trent finally and reluctantly excused herself to join two men who were waiting for her outside the main entrance to the Savoy. On the sidewalk stood an earnest, rail thin, bespectacled, twenty-something reporter for 'Hollywood Chatterbox,' Handy Weather. Calmly watching the rookie scribe rock back and forth from leg to leg, was the aging chauffeur at Miss Trent's service on that part of the circuit, a sharecropper's son and the grandson of slaves. Currently called Clyde, the old fellow used various monikers at different junctures in his life.

A full hour earlier, Clyde had double-parked a bluegray Packard in front of the hotel's entrance, during which time he simply ignored the blooming wrath engendered by the hefty motorcar blocking the trafficway.

Quite like a peppy mongrel pup, Handy Weather was on Pam Ella Trent's heels the moment she set foot onto the sidewalk fronting the Savoy.

"Miss Trent?" Handy blathered.

Spinning around to face Handy, Miss Trent prepared to autograph another paper scrap for a fan.

"I am," she boasted, batting her heavily made up eyes.

"Oh, Miss Trent, I'm Handy Weather."

Pursing her lips, Miss Trent did not understand what the reporter said, unable to hear over the din of yet another horn of a passing auto bearing still one more driver delayed by the offending Packard.

"The weather? Is what?" she asked, plainly irritated.

Cupping his hands over his mouth to form a makeshift bullhorn, Handy Weather repeated his introduction.

Improvidently screaming when the passing motorist ceased laying on the horn, Handy Weather bellowed: "I'm a reporter from 'Hollywood Chatterbox'."

Pam Ella Trent's eyes popped wide open, her face looking quite like a quickly uprighted ceramic doll with movable lids.

"Reporter?" Miss Trent cooed.

"Yes, ma'am. I'm to go with you to Topeka today."

"Oh my, yes," she replied, having no idea what Handy Weather was talking about.

No longer particularly listening to the cub reporter she asked: "'Hollywood Chatterbox', then?"

"Yes, ma'am."

"Delicious," she exclaimed, turning to Clyde the chauffeur.

"Floyd, let's be off."

Clyde courteously tipped his driving cap, ignoring the misnomer, used to being called many names.

Handy followed Miss Trent into the broad, leather rear seat of the Packard. Clyde wasted little time in maneuvering the auto into the flow of traffic. "Now, tell me, Randy ..." "Handy," he corrected.

Miss Trent believed he referred to the ever-ready reporter's notepad that he held rather than correcting her abuse of his name.

"Oh, yes, handy," she replied. "Now, Randy, tell me, will this be a cover story?"

"It's Handy," he repeated.

"Yes, love. It's a handy little pad you have there. So Randy, will this be a cover story?"

Resigned, Handy advised the actress that the piece on her was intended for the cover.

"Delicious," she enthused as Clyde pointed the automobile west towards Topeka.

"My editor and your manager agreed that I can stay with you through your show tonight, backstage, even."

"Of course," Miss Trent firmly responded despite lacking any prior recollection of anything Handy discussed.

The mid-July afternoon was a scorcher. The plains' inferno took a toll on the corn crops. As the Packard sped towards the Kansas capital city, fields on each side of the roadway featured weather weary sentinels: drooping, drying, stalks of corn.

Handy scribbled here and there on his narrow notepad as he chatted with the actress during the seventy-mile motor trek to Topeka.

"So, Miss Trent, you began the circuit in New York?"

"Yes, Andy, we did. We began at the Apollo. It was a delicious start."

"And, you end in Hollywood?"

"Yes. And that will also be delicious."

"And you play thirty cities in between?"

"That's right, Andy."

Miss Trent diverted her attention from the reporter and on towards Clyde in the front seat. "Bradley," she sounded, not getting the driver's attention immediately because of the error in name. She patted on the front car seat to get Clyde's attention.

"Bradley, how long 'til Topeka?"

"About forty-five minutes, Miss Trent," Clyde replied. "Your show is a revue?" Handy asked.

"Yes, a delightful revue. A revue of Broadway tunes from '27, '28, and '29."

"But not this year?" he asked.

"None from 1930, that's right. But all the divine show tunes from '27, '28, and '29." Miss Trent bubbled in her seat, sounding more like a teenage schoolgirl than a sixty-year-old songstress.

"Will you do any films anytime soon?" Handy earnestly inquired of the actress.

With pursed lips, nearly a frown, Miss Trent responded with a terse, "Films?"

"Yes, ma'am."

"Films?"

"Yes, ma'am. Any new films coming up?"

Miss Trent sat motionless, as if a brittle frost had infiltrated the auto and chilled her stony solid. "No," she replied, hardly over a whisper.

"I love your films," Handy noted, with a glowing smile.

Warming up promptly, Miss Trent grabbed onto one of the reporter's hands with both of her own. "You do?" she beamed.

"Oh, yes, Miss Trent. I've seen them all, every one."

"Oh, my, Andy, that's so kind." She feigned embarrassment, held her breath hoping her cheeks would flush.

"You're my favorite, Miss Trent."

"Oh, you're a divine young man."

"I bet your revue is packing them in, Miss Trent."

"Packing ... them in," she hesitated. "Well, yes."

Pam Ella Trent and Handy Weather continued to chat. Handy occasionally scribbling a note or thought on his reporter's pad. Within what seemed like little time to the Packard's passengers, they reached the outskirts of Topeka.

"You know, Randy, the Governor will be at my performance tonight."

"The Governor?"

"Yes, Alf Landon, the Governor. You know, in nearly every state I've performed, the Governor has come."

"I'm not surprised," Handy fawned. "You're just the best"

"Randy, you're so lovely."

Clyde interrupted the conversation between Miss Trent and the reporter for the first time since the auto trip commenced. "We'll be at your hotel in a few minutes, Miss Trent."

"Marvelous. I could use a nap." Turning to Handy, she fluffed her hair and added, "Beauty sleep, you know."

Handy bowed his head, like a shy schoolboy laying an apple on the teacher's desk. "Aw, Miss Trent, you'd be beautiful with no sleep at all."

"You're spoiling me, Andy," she swooned. "I'll never be able to sit for another interview again. Not ever, ever."

"Rupert!" Miss Trent called out to the driver. "Rupert!" she repeated.

"Oh, yes ma'am," Clyde finally replied, realizing he was being called upon.

"Rupert, how far is the hotel from the theater?"

"Right next door, ma'am. Actually connected. Plus, the theater has refrigerated air."

She giggled with delight. "And they say everything's up to date in New York City."

Within a few minutes, the Packard pulled up to the Hotel Jayhawk.

Clyde hurried to open Miss Trent's door and then that of her ride-along guest. She strutted into the lobby with Handy shuffling behind, Clyde hoisting her luggage out of the trunk.

Pam Ella Trent looked obviously disappointed to find the lobby empty except for a bald reservation clerk and a bellman sound asleep on a chair near the main entrance. She snorted, clearly displeased.

"Franklin!" she shouted, again for Clyde. He was quicker on his feet in that instance.

"Ma'am?" he replied, weighed down with the lady's luggage.

"There's no one here," she snapped.

Clyde scoured the lobby, spotting the desk clerk and the dozing bellman. He wondered who else would be necessary. He only wished the bellman was alert and not snoozing. He needed help with Miss Trent's traveling packs.

Handy knew to what Miss Trent referred and shuttled up to her side. "Miss Trent, the folks here obviously didn't know when you were scheduled to arrive or this lobby, this whole city block, would be filled with your people … your fans."

Handy's exuberant style made Miss Trent's face beam.

"Oh, Andy," she gushed, shortly stopping and bestowing full attention on the eager reporter. "You're such a dear."

Handy blushed, scraping the tip of his left shoe across the terrazzo tile floor. Clyde, in the meantime, had reached the reservation service desk and advised the clerk of Miss Trent's arrival. The desk clerk fumbled about clearing some loose papers off the counter. He then licked his fingertips and slid them across the wispy ring of hair on each side of his balding head.

Handy and Miss Trent reached the reservation desk at the moment the clerk finished fiddling with his thin mane.

"Miss Trent," he greeted, his nasal, high pitched, nearly whining voice causing Pam Ella Trent and Handy Weather to actually wince.

"Good afternoon," she replied with flourish.

"I'm so excited to have you here," the clerk went on.

Miss Trent raised her arm and bent her hand forward at her wrist: "Go on."

"Really. And I have a ticket for your show. I got a ticket, I did."

"How wonderful! I am so glad you will be there."

"Me, too! Me, too!" the desk clerk bounced as he spoke.

The clerk turned his attention towards Handy and frowned.

"Do you have a reservation?" he snapped, acting as if Handy Weather invaded his domain.

Handy nodded, grinning. Miss Trent spoke extolling Handy's praises. "He's a reporter for 'Hollywood Chatterbox.' He's doing a story on me … a cover story."

In a condescending way, the clerk snorted: "Oh, a reporter. The press." He wholly refocused on Miss Trent and told the actress the hotel set aside the best suite for her stay.

"Delightful," she replied.

Looking down his nose, over the top of his glasses, the clerk told Handy he would find a room for the reporter. Once he had Miss Trent registered, he clapped his hands sharply twice, bringing around the dozing bellman who moved to the desk as if waiting a command to service and not as a man lumbering in sleep.

The clerk announced Pam Ella Trent as if boasting of a newly obtained and precious possession. "The Jayhawk Suite," the clerk concluded, after which the bellman placed Miss Trent's luggage on a porter's cart.

"Will you need me any more this afternoon?" Clyde diligently inquired.

"No, Emerson. Be back tomorrow in time for me to get to Kansas City and the airfield." Turning to the clerk, she spouted that her next show was the following night in Denver. Facing Handy, Miss Trent rattled: "Then off to Salt Lake, Boise, Seattle, San Francisco, and Hollywood."

"It's great," Handy enthused.

"Yes!" Miss Trent agreed.

"What about my room?" Handy asked of the clerk. The clerk responded by waving him off.

"Take Miss Trent to her suite," the clerk directed the porter, pointing towards the elevators. "If you need anything at all, Miss Trent, you just ring on down. I'll be on duty until your show."

"Wonderful."

The desk clerk asked for Miss Trent's autograph, which she scribbled on a guest ticket. She started off towards the elevators; two double sets of golden doors, the bellman following closely behind.

"Miss Trent," Handy called after the actress.

She spun around, her dress easily twirling. "Yes, Randy?"

"My interview …" his voice trailed off.

94

"Oh, of course dear. You meet me here in the lobby, say, at six tonight. Then we'll go off to my dressing room at the theater and you can do your interview there."

"Great," he eagerly agreed.

Miss Trent stepped into the elevator, leaving the clerk and Handy Weather standing in the lobby with longing eyes like two whelping pups. Clyde grinned wryly and slightly shook his head, making for the door and the shiny Packard.

Ensconced in the heavily appointed suite, Miss Trent quickly abandoned her day clothes and slipped into a lavender silk dressing gown. She poured herself a gin with a spritz of tonic and took a seat on an emerald plush chaise.

Handy was ushered to a simple room on the hotel's second floor. He spent the afternoon sketching penciled pictures of cats, dogs and ducks. The reservation clerk spent the afternoon doodling 'Pam Ella Trent' on guest cards and bellman receipts.

Miss Trent's revue's staging director arrived in Topeka nearly two hours behind the star, stuck in Kansas City dealing with a frustrated costumer who needed to be coaxed, cajoled and finally cleanly bribed to continue with the circuit. He was frantic and irritable when he reached the Jayhawk Theater.

The Jayhawk Theater, nearly ten years old, was a graceful venue. The elaborate décor and resplendent lighting created the perfect environment for traveling vaudevillians, play actors, and other sundry performers who trooped across the heartland. When opened, at a festive gala still well recalled in the Midwestern city, the State Theater of Kansas proudly proclaimed its refrigerated air and fine facilities as making the Jayhawk a 'haven for performers and audiences alike'.

By the time Hartford Wayclocks, the staging director, arrived in Topeka, late, he was so disorganized, perturbed, he stormed into the gaily elegant theater barely taking in any of the accoutrements and trappings. The chilled air, however, braced him like an icy splash.

The Jayhawk Theater's manager nervously waited at the main entrance, a post he maintained for over ninety minutes, anxiously expecting the well-overdue director of Pam Ella Trent's revue. He dramatically gasped, with theatrical relish, when Hartford Wayclocks finally appeared at the show palace.

"Where have you been?" the theater manager asked, trying to hide his anger behind a flat, even Midwestern drone.

"Problems," the life-long New Yorker, with matching accent, snapped.

"Follow me," the theater manager, resigned, prompted. He led Hartford Wayclocks through the plush, dimly lit auditorium up to the stage where redfaced and tiring hands busied themselves setting up for the revue. "Things seem to be getting in order," the manager remarked, doing his best not to sound snide.

"Thank God," Hartford exclaimed, relieved. He imagined the stage and house to be in disarray because of his tardy appearance. "Did Miss Trent stop in?"

"No."

"No?" Hartford, somewhat surprised, asked.

"No." The manager's voice remained as level as a Kansas plain, leaving Hartford unable to determine how the chap felt.

"Is she here?" Hartford asked, meaning in Topeka.

"No," the manager replied, an edge of frustration inching into his voice.

"No?"

"I've told you that, Mr Wayclocks."

"I mean, is she in Topeka?" Hartford clarified.

"I don't know."

"You don't know?"

"I don't."

Muttering to himself, Hartford decided to dash next door to the hotel to see if the leading, indeed the show's *only* lady, had

96

arrived. Without saying another word to the manager, Hartford dismounted the stage and started plodding through the empty house. He turned when he reached the back rows and asked how the house looked for the night.

The manager replied by sticking his arm out straight, hand flat, and tipping his hand slightly from side to side. "So-so," he replied.

"Damn!" Hartford shot, slapping his own thigh before exiting the theater.

While Hartford Wayclocks bustled over to the hotel, Pam Ella Trent poured herself another gin with a dinky dash of tonic water. She opened her cosmetic bag, sifting around until she found a vial of lavender bubble bath, the color matching her silken dressing gown. Making her way to the bathroom, tiled in powder blue, she twisted on the tub's faucet to draw herself a steaming bath. Directly before she plunged into the tub, as she dangled her toes in the water, the telephone in her room clanged to life.

"Rats!" she blurted, quickly retreating from the bathroom, snatching the phone.

"Yes?" she answered.

"Miss Trent?" Hartford Wayclocks asked, phoning from the lobby.

"Yes?" She still did not recognize the director's voice even after several months of rehearsals and performances.

"It's Hartford … Wayclocks," he sighed.

"Love, how are you?"

"What's the matter with the costume for the finale?" he bluntly asked, referring to his battle that morning in Kansas City with the seamstress who almost abandoned ship.

"That's correct," she snipped back.

Not understanding, he asked Miss Trent what she meant.

"Hartford," she purred, "it looks like a costume. It should look like … no, no … it should *be* a gown … a delicious, beaded gown."

"Miss Trent," he sighed, tightly shutting his eyes and then jabbing his eyelids with two fingers. "It is the same dress you've worn in every show since we started the circuit. Why now? Why change now?" "Hartford," she cooed.

"But Miss Trent ..."

"Hartford ..." she interrupted.

"I'll stay on it," he surrendered.

"You're delicious."

At precisely six o'clock, Pam Ella Trent descended on the lift and entered the lobby like a grand dame, gowned in white silk and velvet, bejeweled in dazzling sapphires. Handy Weather stiffly sat on a couch in the lobby, the reservation clerk outside his post scurried across to meet Miss Trent. The bellman, again asleep, lightly snored. A half dozen others, five hotel guests and a lost visiting minister looking for the First Presbyterian Church some five blocks away, idled in the lobby until Pam Ella Trent appeared. They all, including the black clad preacher, swept up to the actress.

Miss Trent spent several minutes taking their praise and writing her name on snips and snatches of paper. She caught sight of Handy, smiling, on the sofa.

"Oh, dear," she told her clutch of fans. "I must go. The press is here, you see. A reporter from 'Hollywood Chatterbox' covering my revue."

She sashayed across the lobby to join Handy.

"Randy!" she greeted, beaming ear to ear.

"Miss Trent," he replied, quickly scrambling to his feet. "You look ... fantastic."

She giggled like a teenaged girl before a summer cotillion. Together they left the hotel and walked to the theater. "We'll visit in my dressing room," she explained to the earnest scribe.

The theater manager, dutifully flitting about the house, escorted Miss Trent and the young reporter backstage to the actress' designated dressing room. A spray of two dozen white roses sat in a crystal vase on a mahogany table in the center of the smallish room. Miss Trent made a beeline at once for the blooms, inhaling a healthy dose of their fragrance.

"Delicious," she sighed.

At the time she arrived, the room was softly lit; the more garish roundabout of white light bulbs surrounding a large makeup mirror remained unlit. Miss Trent graciously asked Handy to join her, to sit with her on a loveseat-sized sofa of burgundy chintz. He propped his ever-present reporter's notepad on his knee and began to interview the star.

The couple spent over an hour discussing Miss Trent's various films and then drifted into a discussion of her early life.

"I'm from West Virginia, you know," she remarked at one point. Handy, in fact, did not.

"Oh, it's true," she said, her gaze drifting off to the white roses and away from Handy Weather.

"I never heard that before," Handy remarked, suddenly flipping through his pages of notes as if the information on Pam Ella Trent's birth and early life might instantly appear in the midst of his scratchings.

"My father ..." she continued, staring at the roses and in a gentle, mellow tone of voice Handy had not yet heard. "Papa ... he mined coal."

Handy stopped flitting through the sheets of notes, put his pen on the sofa, down at his side.

"Mama ... Mama ..." Handy thought, for a fleeting moment, that Miss Trent's eyes nearly pooled in tears. "She passed ... Mama passed on when I was thirteen. I had six older brothers, Andy, and one younger sister."

Miss Trent smiled, a misty look, as if lost in the tender white rose petals.

"Poor ... we were, of course, poor ... lived in a small house, really only two rooms. We lived not so far from Virginia ... that end of West Virginia, in a small town called Galaxy Falls."

99

"I've never heard any of this," Handy mumbled. "The studio says … well, there's nothing of this in what the studio writes about you."

"I imagine not," she knowingly smiled.

"I thought you were from California."

Miss Trent shyly grinned. "For the past twenty years, Randy, I almost believed I was from California myself." "How'd you get there, Miss Trent?"

Sadly, slowly, she explained that her father was killed in a mine fire when she was fifteen. "My brothers were just old enough to be on their own. My sister was just young enough to be terribly innocent, needy you see. But, there I was … lost, really, in the middle of it all."

In Handy's eyes, Miss Trent – Pam Ella – suddenly appeared differently. She seemed vulnerable, gentle, kindly, soft.

Before either Handy or Miss Trent spoke further, a stern rapping came from the other side of the dressing room door.

"Miss Trent?" the man's voice called out.

Once more not recognizing the voice of her show's director, she panned: "I wonder who that could be?"

Just as quickly as her expression and features had become delicate and fragile, she bloomed fully back into Pam Ella Trent, the indomitable star.

She moved to the door with a flurry that belied the rather tight quarters. Popping the door open, she found Hartford Wayclocks standing in front of her.

"Hartford!" she exclaimed, as if not having set eyes on the man for years, rather than hours.

"Miss Trent," he responded, far more subdued. "You know," she puffed, "the press is here."

Hartford looked confused. "Here?" he asked.

"Here," she enthused, gesturing at Handy Weather. "Randy Winter," she incorrectly continued, "my director, Hartford Wayclocks."

Hartford moved towards Handy, who stood and flushed crimson.

"You're with 'The Tattler?'" Hartford asked, referring to a scandal rag.

Handy meekly shook his head. "No."

Hartford barely paid attention to Handy's response, focusing on Miss Trent, who he believed had concocted a story to cover the young man's presence in her dressing room.

"I thought ..." Hartford said to Miss Trent in a paternal tone. "I thought 'The Tattler' reporter met up with us tomorrow in Denver."

"Oh, no, Love, the press is here now," Miss Trent grandly replied, gesturing magnificently at Handy Weather. "He's with 'Hollywood Chatterbox,' Hartford."

Hartford frowned, displeased. Nonetheless, he carried on and asked if everything in the dressing room was satisfactory.

"Aren't the flowers delicious?" she asked. "I've never seen anything like them."

Hartford rolled his eyes to the ceiling. Miss Trent always insisted on two dozen white roses in her dressing room and the buds and blossoms always looked the same. "Right," he muttered.

"Are we sold out again?" she asked.

Pam Ella Trent's revue had not sold out one night during the circuit, Hartford obviously knew.

"No," he tersely responded.

"Well, fiddle-dee-dee," she replied, waving a hand in front of her face. "I'm sure by show time the house will be filled."

She asked Hartford what the time was for curtain. Throughout the entire circuit, curtain was set for eight o'clock each night. Mouthing "eight" directly to Miss Trent, Hartford exited the dressing room, the door slamming behind him.

"I really must prepare," Miss Trent advised when they were left alone.

Handy looked bruised, hurt like a boy child who misplaced his baseball mitt.

"Can we finish this later?" he meekly asked the star.

"Of course! We'll celebrate the show – with Champagne." She directed Handy to return to her dressing room when the curtain fell.

The doors of the Jayhawk opened to the public at seven o'clock. By show time the house ended up threequarters full, a respectable turnout with unreserved arrivals.

The petite orchestra traveling with the revue struck up the overture directly after eight o'clock. As the curtain rose, a solitary spotlight with a blue gel cast a soft circle of light center stage. There stood Pam Ella Trent, resplendent in a sleek satin gown, rose colored, with a blood red boa wrapping her neck and falling down her front and back.

Accepting the applause of her faithful fans with a regal thrust of both arms, hands upward, she then greeted: "Good evening."

The dutiful orchestra struck up the opening tune, which Miss Trent belted out with vim and flare. Fortyfive minutes later, she wound down the first half of her show with a bluesy medley of songs from a Broadway cabaret of 1928.

The curtain fell as the audience stood in ovation. Miss Trent stood center stage with folded hands and head bowed, a prayerful stance. She remained frozen in that position for over ninety seconds after the curtain fell and the house lights went up. She then whisked off stage to her dressing room, lightly moving between crew and props like a dainty sprite.

Hartford Wayclocks waited for Miss Trent directly outside her dressing room door.

"Isn't it a divine night," she gushed, swirling past Hartford into her space. He had to admit the show progressed well, the audience pleased.

A dressmaker's dummy stood square center in the dressing room with a new, replacement gown hanging neatly.

"Better?" Hartford asked, referring to the gown.

"Delicious," she broadly smiled, waving the stage director off so she could re-garb. She wasted no time in putting on the new gown, a crepe and beaded creation in ivory.

During intermission, the gathered theatergoers milled around the lobby, pleasantly discussing their approval of the show.

"She's so elegant," a plump, merry lady of Topeka society remarked to recognized folk time and time again.

"Her gown … majestic," commented another similarly situated woman.

"Her voice, like an angel. Two angels, in fact," the city's Mayor crooned.

"Time of my life," the bare crowned hotel desk clerk told a handsome couple who attended his church.

Within twenty minutes, the lobby lights flashed, the house lights began to dim. The patrons hurried back to their thickly upholstered seats.

The musicians in the pit mounted the overture for the second act, a lightly tuned lead in to Miss Trent's reopening number. The curtain rose with Miss Trent center stage, resplendently illuminated and perfectly poised.

Her performance for the final half of the evening's show was flawlessly made, a perfect presentation in all respects. She rounded out the revue with a finale featuring a rousing showstopper from the hit musical of 1929 on the Great White Way. After the initial curtain call, Miss Trent took three more before the jocular crowd gave way, ending their steady ovation.

Miss Trent retired to her dressing room, awaiting Handy Weather to conclude his interview for the 'Hollywood Chatterbox.' Ten minutes passed before she heard a knock at the door. Expecting the reporter, she instead found Hartford Wayclocks, the Jayhawk Theater manager, and the hotel desk clerk standing beyond the threshold.

Hartford wore a queerly satisfied expression while the manager and the clerk shifted nervously from side to side.

103

"We have news," Hartford piped up.

"Entrez," Miss Trent graciously invited. "The press will be here soon," she added. Hartford smiled at the remark.

"Your reporter friend ..." Hartford said slyly, turning to the theater manager. "What's his name?"

"Weather ... Handy Weather."

"Delightful man," Miss Trent interjected. "And a wonderful reporter. Very successful."

The same impish smile swept over Hartford's face. "Yes, well ..." he replied. "That's our news."

"Oh, Miss Trent," the reservation clerk from the neighboring Hotel Jayhawk blathered. "It's horrible, just terrible."

A baffled look crossed Miss Trent's face. "Yes?" she asked tentatively.

"Your reporter friend," Hartford stated, with definite relish.

"Is Randy all right?" she asked.

"Your reporter friend," Hartford continued as if Miss Trent had not spoken. "He isn't a reporter at all," he said, savoring the moment.

Miss Trent furrowed her brow, raised a finger to her ruby lips.

"It's just horrible," the clerk muttered his earlier mantra.

Hartford chuckled heartily. "Turns out," he stated, almost in a boast, "turns out your friend the reporter, this Handy Weather ... turns out Handy Weather, he walked off from the State Insane Asylum a few days back. Walked away, ended up in Kansas City, ended up playing reporter."

Miss Trent let out a short whimper, quickly covering her mouth fully with the previously poised hand. The desk clerk solemnly shook his head, grieving that the film star had been duped. Trying to boost Miss Trent, he remarked that he "was certain that young fellow was up to no good."

Having almost savagely struck with his news, Hartford casually announced that he and his temporary cohorts would take their leave. Left to herself in the dressing room, Miss Trent methodically changed out of the new gown.

She departed her dressing room, walked across the lonely stage where a man was busy sweeping. Their eyes met and for an instant she brightened like a star. Taking the steps at stage left, she walked through the empty house, through the lobby and out onto the street.

As Pam Ella Trent walked back to the hotel, light snow began to fall.

The Bouillon Cube

"It's what?" Hester DeWayne asked of her gentleman caller, Richard Therese.

Richard, who fancied himself an inventor, regularly paid a call upon Hester DeWayne and had done so for over a year, since the springtime of 1924. On most occasions of his visits, Richard carried along his latest invention, the fruit of his heartfelt tinkerings.

In April of '24, on his first trip to Hester's parlor, Richard Therese brought a Victrola he had somehow rigged up to a gasoline powered engine.

"Just think," he explained after presenting his creation with a flutter of hands and an enthusiastic "tada." "Just think, Miss Hester. With a bucket of gasoline, a Victrola can play on and on without winding once."

"Oh, my," Hester said at the time, clutching a lace hanky to her ample bosom. Hester, then twenty-six, was a full-figured woman with raven hair and chocolate brown eyes. Her father, Clyde, was the local physician in the tiny hamlet of Rossville, Kansas, just ten miles from the state capital city of Topeka.

Unlike Hester DeWayne at barely five feet in height, Richard Therese was tall, lanky, and almost spindly. He was thirty when he presented Hester with the petroldriven Victrola.

"Should I crank it up, Miss Hester?"

"I thought that with gasoline you didn't need to turn the crank," she rejoined, puzzled.

"Ha, ha," he guffawed. "Figure of speech, really. I mean, shall I turn on the Victrola?"

Hester hesitated for a moment, trying to imagine how the contraption might work.

"Come on," he prodded. "It wasn't easy getting it here in the first place."

"Well, all right then," Hester relented.

Within a minute, Richard fired up the engine and had the record-playing machine twirling at top speed, too fast in fact. For a couple of seconds, the tune emitted from the Victrola appropriately, but as the machine picked up speed, the sound pouring out from the solitary scope was akin to that of furious felines of alley cat stock.

In little time, the parlor filled with foul smelling ash gray smoke fuming from the pumping engine.

"Good heavens," Hester yelped, unsure whether she should use her hands to fend off smoke reaching her nose or to cover her ears to block the racket from the music player.

Despite his best efforts, Richard could not shut down the Victrola. Dense smoke ended up billowing from the DeWayne residence on Spruce Park Avenue, bringing round a wagon and crew from the volunteer fire department.

Surprisingly, three weeks later, Hester agreed to another visit from Richard Therese. She cautiously opened the door to her family home, making certain that Richard had no machine, motor or engine in tow. The family's maid had not yet succeeded in cleaning the smoke stains from the parlor walls.

"Come in," she cautiously invited.

In the parlor, they stiffly chatted for half an hour.

"How are you?" Richard asked.

"Fine."

"Good."

"Yes," she concurred.

"I'm well," he remarked.

"Good."

"Yes," agreed Richard. "Your father?"

"Fine."

"Good. And your mother?"

Hester advised: "Well."

"Good."

"Yes." Hester asked about Richard's parents.

"Good."

"Both?"

"Yes."

"Good."

"Yes," he nodded.

After more than thirty minutes of stilted conversation, Richard reached into his suit coat pocket after telling Hester he wanted to "show her something." She thought, on the spot, of dashing off to the kitchen to fetch a pitcher of water. She felt certain Richard was poised to fetch something from his clothing that most likely would spark, smoke or catch fire.

She furrowed her brow, confused, when she caught sight of the two-inch long stick that appeared to be covered with gaily colored paper. He held up the stick, fiddled around with it for a moment. In an instant, the stick transformed into a tiny umbrella, purple, pink and pale blue.

"What's that?" she blurted.

Proudly, Richard explained: "An umbrella."

"Umbrella?"

"Yes, an umbrella."

Hester touched the tiny device. "Paper," she muttered

"What?" asked Richard.

"Paper," she replied. "It's made of paper."

He nodded, beaming brightly. "And colorful." "But, it's paper," she protested. "And too small." "Too small?" he asked.

"Too small. And paper."

"Why ... yes," he finally agreed.

"What good, Richard, is a tiny umbrella made of paper?"

Glum all of a sudden, Richard shrugged and muttered something Hester did not understand.

Despite being flattened by Hester's critique of his diminutive paper and stick umbrella, the visit ended quite well. In Hester's mind, any time with Richard Therese that concluded without the need for fire fighters was well spent.

Richard continued to call on and visit Hester with regularity. By the springtime of 1925, he saw Hester weekly. Hester eventually became used to, or at least not surprised by, the queer and unusual items Richard created. As a result, when he came bearing a half-inch wide flaky, brown cube, Hester was puzzled but nonplussed.

When Hester asked: "It's what?" Richard promptly piped back: "Bouillon." "Bouillon?" she asked.

"Bouillon," he confirmed.

Slowly Hester reached across the coffee table in the parlor where Richard placed the little cube. She lightly touched it with her right forefinger.

"It's what?" she questioned Richard again. "It's bouillon."

"Like … the soup?" she asked.

He nodded.

"But …" she said, hesitating.

"Yes?" Richard replied, sounding encouraging.

"Well, Richard, it's just a square." He nodded.

"A square, Richard."

"Of bouillon," he remarked.

"A square of bouillon?" she squinted her eyes as she spoke and looked again at the solitary cube on the table.

"Yes, Hester. A bouillon square."

Hester sucked in her upper lip, sitting still and quiet for a couple of minutes.

"What do you do with it?" she asked.

"The bouillon square," Richard replied.

She nodded.

Previously, the maid had brought in a tray loaded with hot water in a pot, tea, cups, saucers and wafer thin cookies.

"Let me show you," Richard replied.

He picked up the cube and dropped it into an empty teacup. He handed the china piece to Hester.

"What do I do with this?" she asked.

Richard gestured towards the teapot. "Pour water on it," he advised.

"Do what?" she asked.

"Pour water on it," repeated Richard.

"In the cup?"

"Right, Hester. In the cup."

Hesitating a bit, Hester picked up the teapot and poured the hot water into the cup and over the bouillon cube.

Instantly, the square dissolved and the hot water turned an opaque brown.

Hester gazed into the cup and then looked up at Richard smiling.

"Soup?" she asked.

He said: "Yes." He then asked Hester if she noticed anything else in the cup. Hester took a second glance into the teacup and did see something lying at the bottom.

"What's this?" she asked Richard, keeping her eyes in the cup, trying to better make out what rested at the bottom.

"It was hidden in the square," he explained.

"Hidden?"

"Yes … I made the square of bouillon with … that … inside."

"But what is it?" Hester pressed.

Richard picked up the teacup and drank the bouillon. When he finished, he set the cup back down on the coffee table. He motioned for Hester to look again.

Seeing clearly for the first time what lay at the teacup's bottom, Hester let out a surprised gasp.

"For me?" she cried.

110

"For you," Richard tenderly replied. He picked up the teacup again and tipped it sideways. An engagement ring slipped from the china cup into his hand.

Quickly he wiped the ring dry with a neat linen napkin from the serving tray. Speaking no further, Richard slipped the ring onto Hester's finger.

Sparkle's Gone

My seventh birthday ended up a big stinker. The day started out pretty fine, though. At eight in the morning my mom, dad and grandma Nanna came upstairs into my room, singing 'Happy Birthday,' waking me into what seemed to be a nice summertime day in my little hometown of Strasburg, Virginia.

My mom's mother, grandma Nanna, lived with my folks and me in our three story, tin-roofed house, painted a neat white, just across from the Parker-Fine Funeral Parlor on Oak Street in our little town of a thousand folks.

I never thought much about living across from the funeral parlor until 1967 when I turned seven, the year of my stinky birthday. But after birthday number seven, I would never look across the street from my front lawn the same again.

Mom and Nanna could carry tunes well. They both sang in the Shenandoah Baptist Church choir. All of the Archers in Strasburg, my family and my kin, went to worship every Sunday morning at Shenandoah Baptist. My dad did not sing with the Shenandoah Baptist Church choir because he was a musical fright. Despite his rotten-sounding singing, he was always the loudest even at Sunday services when the pretty-sounding choir sang, and certainly when my folks and Nanna woke me to the 'birthday song.' Dad also got the words to songs mixed all up most times. On my sixth birthday, Mom and Nanna smoothly sang:

"Happy birthday to you!
Happy birthday to you!
Happy birthday Dear Clay!
Happy birthday to you!"

Dad, on the other hand, loudly managed:

"Happy day Clay!

Birthday to you!
Happy! Birthday!
Dear Clay!
To you"

Very loudly.

My dad's scratchings actually roused me from sleep, alarmed and terrified, until I saw the happy expressions of my family and realized the racket was only Dad trying out a song.

I scrambled out of bed after the bedroom concert, scrubbed my face and teeth, pulled on short pants and a clean T-shirt. Within the hour, three of my buddies would be over at our house; Kenny Walker, Patrick Jonas and Shoe Landeau. Shoe's name was really Mark. When we were in kindergarten the year before, Mark religiously put his shoes on the wrong feet after naptime, gaining the nickname 'Shoe,' thought up by Patrick Jonas himself. All the adults called Patrick Jonas 'clever,' Kenny Walker 'trouble,' and me 'nice.' Adults did not say much about Shoe, other than "he really tries, huh?"

Shoe's papa actually went to the Parker-Fine Funeral Home when we four boys were in kindergarten. Shoe's papa went boozing at the Harvest Pub in town and ended up getting smashed by a train after passing out on the railroad tracks while trying to walk home.

After I dressed, I wasted no time getting downstairs for breakfast and to wait for the arrival of my buddies. Because it was a weekday, the very first part of July, Dad had to go to work even though I was out of school for the summertime. Dad sold auto insurance from an office on Main Street in Strasburg. Nearly everyone in town who drove got their auto insurance from Dad, except for a spinster lady named Priscella Wayclocks whose house we all avoided on Halloween and when selling greeting cards for the school PTA. Even though our parents tagged along,

113

except for Shoe's papa who was run down by the 525 to Baltimore, we never went to Priscella Wayclocks' front door.

Some of the older boys, from Mamie Dowd Eisenhower Junior High, did toss toilet paper into Miss Wayclocks' trees at the start of summer. I was surprised when the toilet paper did not burst into flames considering the witch us younger kids thought lived inside that house at the end of Maple Road, Miss Wayclocks.

Dashing into the kitchen on my birthday for breakfast, Nanna blurted out: "Our big boy!"

She said that, even though I was about the shortest boy in my school class, except for Freddy Tender. Folks around Strasburg said Mr Tender, Freddy's pop, still made moonshine even though it really wasn't necessary with package stores and all. Pastor Crimshaw's wife from Shenandoah Baptist Church said about old man Tender: "You can take some people out of the hills, but you can't take the hills out of some people."

I didn't know what Mrs Crimshaw meant by that, but I guessed it had something to do with the Tenders coming from West Virginia and their having a still in their back yard and a 1948 Ford pickup truck in front, propped up on cement blocks. Anyway, Freddy Tender wasn't coming over for my birthday.

After Nanna proclaimed me a 'big boy' in the kitchen, my Dad piped up: "He sure as cotton is a big fellow." Dad's speaking voice was just fine, not rottensounding like the way he sang.

My mom, not to be left out, piped in: "My little man."

After she said her bit, she held up a plate heaped high with pancakes.

"Look, little man," she said, looking like a magazine model advertising a griddle. "Hotcakes!"

She put the platter of golden brown cakes on the table, where she'd already set out bacon, sausage, chopped up grapefruit and buttered grits.

We were all eating when Shoe and his mother, a woman my Mom called mousey, showed up on our front porch, lightly knocking on the door.

"I bet that's Mrs Landeau and Shoe," Mom said.

"Why doesn't she use the bell?" Dad asked.

Whispering, leaning forward and acting like Mrs Landeau could hear through brick walls, Mom replied: "She's mousey … very mousey."

"I'll get it," I declared, jumping from the table and making for the door in a split second. I lead Shoe and his mousey mother into our kitchen. When Mrs Landeau saw Mom, Dad and Nanna sitting around the table crammed with food, I thought the woman was going to faint. I really saw the color just wash right out of her face. She gasped: "Oh, Lordy … we're early!" She looked directly down at Shoe. I thought, at first, she was checking to see if he had everything on the right foot. "Mark, I thought you said we should be here at nine o'clock?"

Before Shoe spoke, Mom got to her feet saying: "It's fine, fine!" She told them both to join us. Shoe looked to be about ready to take a chair when Mrs Landeau spoke.

"No, no. We've eaten."

She spoke in such a way that I imagined she thought Mom believed the Landeaus to be charity cases in need of food with Shoe's pop being squished by a train and all.

"Nonsense," Mom quickly replied. "Sit. Have some coffee, juice at least."

Mom shuffled off to the cabinet to retrieve fresh plates for Shoe and Mrs Landeau. I kept my eyes on Mrs Landeau who kept her own on Mom. Mrs Landeau looked like she didn't know whether to sit, run off or puke her guts out from nerves. She finally sat and I took to eating my pancakes again.

Mom dished up healthy servings for Mrs Landeau and for Shoe. They both looked at their plates like Mom handed over Martian food for them to eat. I figured Mrs Landeau felt she was

115

being impolite interrupting our breakfast and felt impolite if she did not eat and had no idea what to do. I figured Shoe plain, flat out had no idea what to do.

Mrs Landeau finally poked at her eggs and, on seeing her move, Shoe dove in, finishing off a couple of hot cakes in nothing flat.

"When will you be back?" Mrs Landeau asked Mom after a few minutes.

"Oh, probably about nine or ten tonight. You know, the boys are just sleeping here."

Mrs Landeau nodded. I looked over at Shoe who was slurping on eggs.

"Can you believe it?" I asked my pal.

"Huh?" he asked, a glob of egg falling out of his mouth.

"Gross," I smacked. Shoe blushed. Mrs Landeau, taking it in – flopping yellow eggs and all – looked like she was about to faint.

Shoe mumbled an apology and I asked him again if he could believe our imminent good fortune.

When my other two buddies arrived, Mom was driving us off to Washington, DC an hour and a half away. Once there, we were off to the WWBC television studios to be on the 'Sparkle the Clown Show.' After that, pizza pies at 'Little Roma Pizza Palace' in Georgetown. Kids having birthdays and their pals got to sit in the audience and get introduced on the 'Sparkle the Clown Show.'

Shoe nodded and smiled, a shy boy's agreement that we had a grand adventure ahead.

Our breakfast group had nearly finished the meal when the front doorbell sounded. I darted out of the kitchen to greet the callers who turned out to be Patrick Jonas and his mother. Kenny Walker and his Mom were pulling up to the curb in front of our house at that very moment.

Within an half an hour, the visiting mothers were going their own ways and Mom was hauling Patrick, Kenny, Shoe and me down Interstate 66 to

116

Washington, DC. We spent the first forty miles of our journey debating pizza toppings for that night's suppertime treat. Each of us boys favored a different topper and finally decided we would each choose one item when time came for supper.

Before noon we were motoring across the Roosevelt Bridge into downtown DC. We needed to be at the WWBC studio by two o'clock and Mom decided she needed to feed us boys. Mothers and food. Mothers and sleep. Mothers and baths. At least us guys enjoyed eating, especially getting meals out, which was a rare treat.

Mom was one of a handful of women in Strasburg in 1968 with a college degree. She spent four years at Georgetown University in DC and knew Washington well. She drove us to a sandwich shop on Capitol Hill, eventually finding a parking space not too far from the diner.

"Maybe we'll see the President," Shoe stupidly said as we walked down the sidewalk toward the sandwich place.

"Yeah, right," Patrick snorted, with all the boyish indignity he could muster.

"We might," Shoe plodded.

"Yeah, right," Patrick retorted, his tone remaining the same.

"If I saw him, I'd kick him right in the nuts," Kenny blurted out, earning a swift, "Kenny, your language, please," from my Mom.

Kenny's brother Billy was off in Viet Nam. I figured he could kick LBJ wherever he saw fit because of all that war stuff and his brother having to fight and all.

When we reached the deli, Mom made us take seats at a table covered by a blue and white checkerboard patterned cloth, while she went to the counter. Knowing Mom, I understood that she did not want to endure four boys at the order stand trying to make up their minds on what to eat. Plus, we likely would each pick malteds and pie slices and nothing more.

117

Before too long, she joined us with a tray of sandwiches. A high school-aged girl who worked at the deli followed behind, wobbling a tray of sodas.

As we ate, our talk turned to the 'Sparkle the Clown Show.'

"Can you believe it?" I asked my pals again.

"Sparkle the Clown has been on TV since 1952," Patrick smartly advised.

"Maybe I'll kick him in the nuts then," Kenny pounded out for no obvious reason other than to nicely rile up Mom.

She did not disappoint and admonished my buddy with a seemingly stern: "Kenny … your mouth … please."

Shoe asked: "Does a clown even have nuts?"

The other three of us, plus even Mom, laughed.

Before long, we all piled back into the car and headed off to WWBC. We were at the television studios in no time at all.

Not one of us four boys really knew what to expect of a television studio. We imagined quite a grand place, considering the importance of the work that went on there.

When Mom pulled the car off the road into the parking lot next to a building that looked like nothing more than a nearly windowless concrete rectangle, we assumed she was lost. I asked: "Are we lost?"

A bit of an edge existed in my voice, fearing we might end up being late for the show.

"We're here," she replied.

"Here?" I asked, puzzled.

Patrick followed my tone and wondered aloud: "You mean this is a TV studio?"

Kenny was looking around, possibly for nuts to kick. Shoe, having no concept of anything, was unfazed by our arrival at the gray concrete rectangle.

"Come on, boys," Mom directed, ushering us out of the car and down a concrete sidewalk that was the same dull color as the entire building itself.

118

Much to my surprise, and that of my three pals, when we walked into the studio building, we found ourselves in a warm looking reception area. I guess we all expected more concrete, probably even concrete furniture. Instead, the reception room had comfylooking sofas, chairs and tan shag carpeting that looked brand new.

In an instant, the receptionist directed us down a hallway which led us to a door outside studio number four where a line of other kids and parents was forming, waiting to enter into the happy domain of Sparkle the Clown.

After we stood in the line not moving for several minutes, I complained to Mom that if we didn't get inside soon, we'd miss the whole show. An old man in an ill-fitting guard's uniform sat in a chair next to the door. While Mom assured me we would be inside the studio in plenty of time for the start of the show, Kenny looked at the guard idling doorside.

Kenny then leaned over and whispered to me: "I can kick him in the nuts."

He pointed towards the old fellow at the entrance. I giggled in response. Patrick tugged on my shirt wanting to know what Kenny said. Shoe was rocking back and forth in a manner that I knew meant he needed to pee. Looking at Shoe shifting around, I panicked.

"Good God," I blurted, repeating a phrase I heard Nanna use with some frequency.

"Clay!" Mom scolded, not pleased yet also puzzled. "What's wrong?" I pointed at

Shoe.

"What?" Mom asked, following the course of my directing finger.

"What?" she asked again.

Sounding rather like a parent himself, Patrick explained that Shoe needed to use the toilet.

"And we're gonna miss the whole show!" I moaned.

Quite like a ballet dancer I once saw, Mom grabbed a hold of Shoe by the hand and seemed to float down the hall back towards the reception area. She turned back to Kenny, Patrick and me as she walked on and told us to save a couple of seats if she did not make it back with Shoe by the time the doors opened.

"They're never gonna make it," I groused to my remaining pals. "They're gonna miss Sparkle and the whole show."

"I should've kicked him in the nuts," Kenny said, being the one who made good sense at the moment.

Calmly, Patrick with his still father-like tone told us that he was sure Mom and Shoe would be back with us in plenty of time. He proved correct. And as if on cue, the old, rumpled guard opened up the door and began ushering the folks in line inside Sparkle the Clown's television studio.

Edging down the hallway closer to the door, I actually could feel my heart pounding in my skinny chest. I wanted to tell Mom and my pals how excited I felt; wanted to tell them about my hard-thumping heart. But, I just couldn't speak, not a single word.

Entering the studio, I gasped, my eyes darting from the stage and set that I had seen so often on my television at home to the three big broadcast cameras to the cluster of lights hanging from the ceiling. Most of all, I was immediately hit by how the studio felt. A blast of cold air greeted my Mom, my pals and me when we walked into the cavernous room. I shivered, my Mom catching the reflex.

She leaned over and explained to my buddies and me: "With all the lights and equipment and whatnot, they have to keep the studio very cool."

Learning these television secrets, which my very own Mom knew well was a moment of pride for me in the eyes of my mates. We took our seats in the studio and good ones we had, right up front, almost in the center.

"This is so great!" I exclaimed.

Patrick, Kenny and Shoe all agreed. I'm sure Mom did too even though she got busy talking to another mother seated next to her.

For nearly ten minutes, the four of us boys kept our eyes peeled on the stage waiting for Sparkle the Clown to bound on out. We expected to hear Sparkle's happy:

"Hey, ho, boys and girls … A hippy dippy to ya!"

And then we would say: "A hippy, dippy to ya, Sparkle!"

And we'd be saying it right in front of Sparkle, right on television, for the whole world to see. Even if it wasn't the whole world, it would at least be greater Washington, DC and parts of Maryland and Virginia, Mom explained in the car on the trip to the studio. She assured me everyone in Strasburg could get – *would* get – the broadcast.

Ten minutes passed, which seemed like ten years to me. I said: "Mom, if this show doesn't start rolling, I'll be an old man … I'll be seventeen before long."

Mom laughed, finding something or another humorous despite my most serious tone.

"It'll be fine," she assured.

"But Mom, the time," I pointed at my trusty Timex, a Christmas gift from the year before from Grandma Nanna that I wore to all major events like trips to be on television.

Before Mom could say 'It'll be fine' again, she looked at my watch, then her own. At about the same time, I became aware of similar rustlings around the studio.

"You know," Mom said, realizing as I did that it was show time, in fact two or three minutes past show time. And the 'Sparkle the Clown Show' broadcast live.

The murmuring all around us increased, and one particularly boisterous mother blurted out for all to hear: "What's going on around here?"

I was most happy that my Mom did not grouch out loud like that woman. Before any one of the other mothers piped up too much, a pudgy, bald man with tiny round glasses, who was obviously

121

sweating despite the polar temperatures, squirmed uncomfortably onto the stage. The entire audience piped down as if the little man on the stage had asked us to be quiet.

From where I sat in the good seats down front, I could see the man's eyes dart back and forth, right and left, like a white mouse in a cage in Mrs Grimm's classroom back at school. He finally spoke: "Boys and girls ..." he began, and then cleared his throat. I figured if he had a frog in his voice he should have cleared it out before he walked onto Sparkle's stage in front of all of us kids and our moms.

"Boys and girls ..." he said again, wiping sweat off his forehead with the back of his hand.

Kenny mumbled: "Gross." And I agreed by nodding.

"Boys and girls ..." he sputtered for a third time. "I have news ..." He shook his head. Mom mumbled to the woman next to her:

"I bet it's the President, just like with Kennedy."

"Bad news," the fellow went on. "Sparkle's ... Sparkle's ..."

The bald man on the stage gave out a mighty sigh.

"Sparkle's gone," he blurted.

"Where to?" I asked Mom in a heartbeat. She furrowed her brow and put a forefinger to her lips, seeming sure the little bald fellow would say more.

"Sparkle's gone," he said again. Tightly shutting his eyes, he spoke further. "Sparkle's passed on."

Horrified gasps and dismayed moans filled the auditorium. At that moment, my seventh birthday ended up a big stinker. But, I remained calm and still.

The pudgy, bald man repeated "Sparkle's passed on" a second time as if us kids hadn't heard the rotten fish news the first time. Mom looked like she was ready to clamp her hands over my ears like she did when bad speaking adults said something nasty in my presence.

122

All of a sudden Shoe Landeau burst into tears. He was the first kid in the whole place to cry and he turned out to be the only boy who really cut loose. I figured Kenny Walker would do some nut kicking if Shoe didn't shape up.

I leaned over to my Mom and whispered in her ear: "What do we do now?" I then added, as if my mom was somehow oblivious to the racked and sobbing Shoe: "Shoe's crying Mom."

"I know, I know," she said, speaking to me using a different tone than I had ever heard her use with me prior to that day. Stunned, nearly, by her inflection, her manner of speech, I asked: "What?"

Mom naturally thought I had not heard her and said: "I said, I'm not sure." The tone remained the same. "I think we need to get Shoe out of here."

"We?" I asked as I came to understand the reason for my Mom's vocal shift, her change in style. She had taken me into her confidence that day. On my seventh birthday, on the set of the Sparkle the Clown Show, I grew up a little in my own mother's eyes, and in my own.

"We need to calm Shoe down," Mom somberly said. "Let's get out of here."

With some effort, Mom and I were able to cajole Shoe out of his seat. Kenny and Patrick were at the door in no time. I overheard Kenny suggest to Patrick that they sneak backstage to see if they might happen upon Sparkle, or what was left of the dead clown.

With my newfound status in Mom's eyes, I was not pleased to hear the boys' conniving. I scowled my disapproval, which I was certain registered with Patrick and Kenny.

By the time we reached my mom's car, Shoe had pulled himself together, more or less.

I retook my seat in the front passenger spot, where I had ridden into the city earlier that day. But on this occasion, I felt different. I felt older, almost more like a person of my Mom's age than a squirrelly boy like Shoe.

Although my seventh birthday ended up a stinker with Sparkle croaking off and all, I took my first, tentative step on a long walk that eventually led me out of boyhood.

There were still plenty of rafting trips left down the Shenandoah River with my pals. There was camping and other happy adventures in the woods of the Massahutten Mountains near home. There were other birthday parties. And, alas, there were even more than a few times when I cried, sometimes kind of like Shoe Landeau at the Sparkle the Clown show.

But, I was on my way.

Thanksgiving Callers

"Damn it, Ma!" I blurted at breakfast, sure that I sounded very adult.

"Kenneth Walker!" she shot back. I avoided her eyes and looked over to Pa who continued to shovel scrambled eggs in his puss as if Ma and I were not debating the merits of walking to Main Street to see the Thanksgiving Day Parade at noon.

Ma continued to speak, rapid fire, and directed her word flow squarely at my choice of language.

"A twelve-year-old boy does not use such language!"

When it came to Ma, a twelve-year-old boy like me pretty much did nothing, and anything I did was probably done incorrectly.

"Isn't that right, Russ?" she asked of Pa.

He obligingly nodded, continuing to stuff his cheeks with egg lumps.

"See, listen to your father," Ma said, referring to a man who never spoke. Listen to her, certainly, but Pa was a man of three words: 'Amen' at church; 'Yep' on occasion; and, 'Nope' once in a while.

"Why do I hafta go?" I asked, redirecting Ma to the real issue, lugging out to the parade.

"Your sisters want to go," Ma said, while three redheaded girls nodded madly at once. My sisters were all younger than me and looked like miniature versions of Ma. We had one older brother – Billy – who could not be home for Thanksgiving. Billy, the serviceman, was off in Viet Nam, some place a zillion miles from our town of Strasburg, Virginia.

"Your brother would go if he were here." Ma made her second point. When reasoning with me, when scolding me, Ma regularly pointed out what she imagined Billy would or would not do if present. I wondered …

"And, young man, we always go to the Thanksgiving Parade, don't we?"

I wanted to say 'damn it' again, or perhaps unfurl a new word I'd learned along the way in Junior High School. Instead, I groaned to make my point.

As it turned out, my point was not made as Ma spat out, just before sipping some homemade apple juice: "Good, I'm glad that's settled."

I matched my groan, to no avail whatsoever, finished my eggs, my sausage and retreated to my room for the inevitable trip up town for the parade.

The Strasburg, Virginia of my youth was a snug, homey hamlet nestled in the Shenandoah Valley. By the age of twelve I pretty much knew everyone in town by name, due in no small part to the fact that there were not many folks to name.

Truth be told, I enjoyed the Thanksgiving Parade. I liked all of our town's parades and the folk of Strasburg marched whenever possible: Memorial Day, Independence Day, Labor Day, Halloween,

Thanksgiving, Christmas and, since I turned ten, even Easter. The parades were all about the same, only the colors changed. Marchers and floats, for example, were well decorated in red, white and blue on Independence Day; orange and black at Halloween; green and red at Christmas; and, most recently, pink and yellow at Easter.

Parade day gave me an extra chance to pal around with my chums up town when, otherwise, the entire day would have found me stuck at home with my folks, my sisters, and, by mid-afternoon, my grandparents in two sets and Pa's unmarried sister, Floreen.

Despite my actually liking the parade (if the truth was told, which I ensured would not happen), I was twelve, I was a boy. I felt in the same way Ma bitched over my language, Pa spent few words, my sisters giggled stupidly and served invisible tea to raggedy dolls, I was supposed to consistently gripe about family

126

outings to civic events. We played our roles and life flowed smoothly through the valley, running evenly like the Shenandoah River in usually placid ways.

We ended up leaving home at 11:30 to make sure Ma was in plenty of time to glom onto her favored parade-watching spot at Main and Third. The parade route, always the same, ran from the post office at Main and First to the Cavendash Feed Store at Main and Eighth. Because the route was so short, the town fathers' – and in 1961 Strasburg like all of Virginia was tightly run by the men folk – horses trotted all through the marching line with rarely a mishap. My chums and I always hoped for mishaps. The best being when Old Man Twilliger's palomino pooped directly on Mayor Jeanette's wife's leg. Mrs Jeanette ended up screaming like a fright, so much so that the palomino spooked and bolted through the crowd and was not caught for two days. All this hoo-haw occurred at the first Easter parade, and I was amazed when another such event occurred the following year.

I spent the hour and some minutes up town during the parade festivities clowning around with my chums Shoe Landeau, Patrick Jonas and Clay Archer. We watched little of the marching and the floats and the Strasburg High School Marching Patriots.

I was home an hour before Aunt Floreen appeared on our doorstep. I answered her buzz on the doorbell and found her dressed true to form on the porch. She wore a red and black plaid skirt, like something I'd seen Catholic girls wear at the picture show in Richmond. Topping the skirt, Aunt Floreen wore a bright orange shirt with a strange tea-colored stain nearly covering one of the sleeves. Perhaps a coffee mishap, I thought. Or perhaps Aunt Floreen had some sort of run in with Old Man Twilliger's palomino.

On her feet, Aunt Floreen wore light blue shoes covered in sequins. She wore no stockings and her legs seemed nearly as pale blue as her shoes, absent the shimmer of the glittering pieces.

127

"Hello, Aunt Floreen," I greeted.

"Kenny, Kenny, Kenny," she said, poking me lightly on the tip of my nose each time she spoke my name.
"How is my toodle-caboodle?"

I assumed she meant her butt and I was about ready to ask her to spin around so I could take a look when Ma appeared at my side.

"He's just fine," Ma replied, I guessed to the toodlecaboodle question. I did not figure out that I was the toodle-caboodle until Ma patted my head.

"Damn it, Ma!" I blurted, intending to stand my ground and tell them both "I ain't no damned toodlecaboodle, and I ain't liking this head patting crap none either."

"Kenneth!" Ma immediately scolded, leaving me little time for anything else but speedy retreat into the living room where Pa adjusted the TV's rabbit ears to get ready for the football games to be shown. I escaped Ma, who fortunately was preoccupied with final preparations for dinner. My four grandparents, to a one, insisted that the holiday meal be served within a quarter hour of their arrival. They drove to our house together, both couples living about ten miles south on the Valley Pike in Woodstock, a town mostly like Strasburg.

I did not, however, escape Aunt Floreen. Off somewhere in the house I heard her calling, "Kenny?" and then again, "Kenny?" For a moment, I felt like we were playing 'Marco Polo,' but rather than respond "Polo" or "In here, in the living room, Aunt Floreen," I hung quietly with Pa who I knew would keep his lips zipped.

I wondered where my sisters had disappeared to. Before I figured out a destination beyond the living room where I could hide until dinner, Pa's sister entered the living room.

"There you are ..." she said, scratching her butt. If Ma saw that she would have made Aunt Floreen wash her hands before turkey. She plopped down on the divan, a heavy but not truly fat woman. She patted the divan next to where she took a seat.

"Come sit by me, Kenny-goo."

"Kenny what?" I asked, turning to Pa for relief. He seemed to be paying no attention, busy as he was with the rabbit ears.

"Come, come … my Kenny-goo." She patted the divan again.

Mumbling "ah, shucks" and "damn it," I slid in next to Aunt Floreen. "If only Billy was here," I thought. "If only Billy was home, he'd know what to do." Seven years older than I was, at nineteen, I believed Billy held all the answers to life's problems.

"So, Kenny-goo, how's school? Are you keeping with your studies?" Aunt Floreen's manner of speaking was classic Confederate or something of the sort.

"Yes'um, Ma'am," I replied, finding myself talking with a twang more distinct than my usual.

"Doesn't the house smell plum yummy, Kenny-goo?"

She was right about that, the smell of dinner in the making all over the house. Thanksgiving Day, and the smell of roasting turkey, fresh pumpkin pie, wheat flour rolls and everything else made me imagine what God's kitchen in Heaven was like everyday.

"Yes'um, Ma'am," I continued in my hypersoutherness, perhaps trying to match Aunt Floreen's own. "It all smells right nice." Deciding to try to draw Pa into my situation with Aunt Floreen, I asked over to him: "Ain't that right, Pa?"

Whether he paid attention or not to developments between Aunt Floreen and me, he said "Yep," and continued messing with the rabbit ears. They'd been adjusted once, but then he moved his chair and now the picture was fuzzy again.

"Well, that's my special Kenny-googly-goo-goo-goo," Aunt Floreen blathered.

Aunt Floreen then asked me for a report on the parade.

"It was … nice," I said, not wanting to share with her the antics of my chums and me while folks dressed like gobblers strutted and clucked up Main Street.

"I didn't make it this year. I was occupied picking out my outfit for today," Aunt Floreen explained. Looking her over once again as she sat on the divan, I imagined a blind hobo could do a far better job of pulling together a wardrobe.

"And Billy? Have you heard from Billy?" she asked.

The mention of my brother's name brought a surprising "Yep" from my Pa who only just finished his fiddling with the television.

"Yes'um, Ma'am," I added, letting her know we got a letter from him on Tuesday. "How is he?" she asked.

"He's doing right well, Ma'am. Fighting the Gooks," I said.

Pa frowned at me, disliking my choice of language, I was sure. I muttered: "I mean the Viet Nam guys."

"Well, Kenny-doodles, Billy boy'll be home soon," Aunt Floreen said with the same tone of voice my math teacher used explaining fractions.

"Yes'um," I replied as the doorbell rang. Saved by the grandparents and a meal that would be served within fifteen minutes. Indeed, we were all around the table in just over ten minutes. Ma led us in a blessing.

"Dear Lord in Heaven, we thank You today. We thank You for our food, this meal. But mostly, Dear Lord, we thank You for our family gathered here today. And, Lord, we ask You to watch over our Billy fighting for freedom and so far from home. Keep him safe, Lord. Amen."

The rest of us, Pa included, said "Amen."

About halfway through dinner, our doorbell rang again.

"Oh, heavens," Ma said, "I just bet that's Miss Grace. Who else could be calling on Thanksgiving?"

"Miss Grace" was Grace Plodden from next door, whose family ate Thanksgiving dinner in the evening.

"She said she was gonna bring over one of her gooseberry pies," Ma added. "You all just sit tight and keep on eating."

Ma got up and hurried out of the dining room to the front door. None of us paid any more attention to the doings in the entryway to our house, all of us preoccupied with the delicious spread in front of us.

A few minutes later, Ma walked into the dining room looking like a ghost with red hair. A couple of seconds later, a middle-aged man in a crisp army uniform came up from behind her.

Aunt Floreen was the first to start crying. My sisters and I looked at each other confused. The fellow in the army uniform softly said: "I'm so sorry."

And then I knew. For a fleeting moment before my eyes filled with tears, I thought of Billy at God's door like the Army guy calling at our own. I pictured Billy sitting in God's kitchen in Heaven having some turkey, some yams and a fresh piece of pumpkin pie.

The End

Biography of Mike Broemmel

Mike Broemmel began writing professionally in 2000 after spending much of his adult life in the political arena. He began his career working in the White House for President Ronald Reagan.

In recent years, Broemmel has enjoyed success as a critically acclaimed, award-winning playwright. His accolades include receiving a grant for his work from the U.S. National Endowment for the Arts and the inclusion of his play *Stand Still & Look Stupid: The Life Story of Hedy Lamarr* in the 2019 Féile an Phobail (the largest arts festival in Northern Ireland). Other award-winning plays by Mike Broemmel include *Goddess People*, *The Row*, *The Baptism*, *Taking Tea with the Ripper*, and *Call Me Mrs. Evers*.

The latest stage plays from Mike Broemmel are *The Wind is Us: The Death that Killed Capote,* about iconic author Truman Capote, which is slated to premiere in 2021. In addition, Mother! - premiered in 2020 and chronicles the life of hell-raising labor leader Mother Jones.

More information about Mike Broemmel and his work is available at www.mikebroemmel.com.

Other Titles by Mike Broemmel

The Shadow Cast – 15th Anniversary Edition
The Miller Moth – 20th Anniversary Edition
Stolen Light
Vine Dancing

Available at: www.mikebroemmel.com.

Made in the USA
Middletown, DE
04 November 2022

14032234R00080